Caribou's Gift

Kodiak Point, Book Four

Eve Langlais

Copyright © August 2014, Eve Langlais
Cover Art by Aubrey Rose © August 2014
Edited by Devin Govaere
Copy Edited by Amanda L. Pederick
Produced in Canada

Published by Eve Langlais
1606 Main Street, PO Box 151
Stittsville, Ontario, Canada, K2S1A3
http://www.EveLanglais.com

ISBN-13: 978-1988 328 34 8

ALL RIGHTS RESERVED

Caribou's Gift is a work of fiction and the characters, events and dialogue found within the story are of the author's imagination and are not to be construed as real. Any resemblance to actual events or persons, either living or deceased, is completely coincidental.

No part of this book may be reproduced or shared in any form or by any means, electronic or mechanical, including but not limited to digital copying, file sharing, audio recording, email and printing without permission in writing from the author.

Chapter One

You know Boris and Travis,
and Brody and Reid,
Guys who kick butt and go to extremes.
But do you recall,
The most vain ex-soldier of all?

The answer was spoken firmly. "No way. Not happening. Never in a million years." Reid could ask all he wanted, but Kyle refused to abase himself that way. A buck had his pride and a duty to his man card after all.

"Aw, come on. Think of the children," Reid, his clan alpha, cajoled.

"Think of me!" Kyle exclaimed. "Do you grasp what you're asking?"

Mirth sparked in his friend's gaze. "Yes. And I know it's not an easy mission. Nor a pleasant one."

"Why not add humiliating and emasculating to the list? I won't do it. I'd rather you punished me."

As leader of the clan overseeing all who resided in Kodiak Point, Reid could very well punish Kyle for his refusal. But in this instance, Kyle wouldn't budge. *Bring on the punishment.*

It wasn't his fault the town was one reindeer short for the upcoming Santa Claus parade. An older, domestic buck had the nerve to croak a few days early leaving them with a team of eight instead of the needed nine. So of course, everyone looked to him. He had to admire the size of his alpha's balls that Reid would dare ask him to take the open spot in the team pulling Santa's sleigh. Admire but still refuse.

Pretend he was a reindeer indeed. Caribou were majestic creatures compared to that simple minded, domestic beast. But there were some people—*good thing they're my friends or I'd have to kill them*—who seemed to think it was okay to ask him to play the part of one just because he possessed a rack. So did a moose, but he didn't see anyone asking Boris if he wanted the part. Then again, the fuse on Boris' temper was pretty short. He'd probably shoot anybody who asked.

Mission #732: Improve my reputation as a badass so people don't make stupid requests.

To those who wondered, while some preferred keeping mental notes, Kyle resorted to thinking of things in terms of missions, a throw over from his military days. Some he completed successfully, such as Mission #713, getting Betty-Sue to give him a piece of her famous apple pie. Success! Others he failed, like Mission #714, his attempt at getting a second piece resulting in bruised knuckles from her infamous wooden spoon.

Travis, Reid's younger cousin and son to the indomitable Betty-Sue, tried to help. "Dude, it's not that bad. Think of it as an acting role."

The bear cub knew to duck before Kyle's fist connected. A shame. "Acting is for—"

"Woodland creatures and humans. So you keep saying," Reid repeated with a roll of his eyes. "You know, I could order you."

"I'd prefer to get my ass handed to me by a bear." He'd rather take a beating than deal with the laughter of his buddies. Ex-army soldiers did not dress up as reindeer with tinsel in their antlers, flashing lights embedded in their harness to pull a sled with a much-too-jolly walrus, who didn't need a fake beard to play the part.

"Scrooge."

"Guilting me won't work," Kyle replied dryly.

"Says you."

"Yes, says me. I don't feel the least bit guilty about saying no. I'm sure the sled will be fine with only eight deer pulling it."

"I can't believe you'll deprive them of the most famous reindeer of all."

"Bite me."

"Ha, like I'd waste my palate on a tough and conceited beast like yourself. But I will throw you to the wolves or, in this case, a cougar," Reid stated.

"What's that supposed to mean?"

"I'm talking about you explaining your refusal to Crystal."

"Who the hell is Crystal?"

"She's a recent newcomer to our town and willing volunteer—"

"Because she didn't know any better," Travis snickered.

"—in charge of making the parade happen. I'm going to let you explain to her why your vanity is more important than doing your part for the children of the community."

Tell a cougar he wasn't going to play the part of a stupid reindeer? "No problem."

Reid slapped him on the back. "If you say so, my brave friend."

Implication? A cougar with too much attitude. Still not an issue. He could handle any old biddy.

I'll just tell her there's no way...

Hello there. A pretty shiny thing entered his line of sight, and all thought left his suddenly blood-deprived brain. Well, all intelligent thought disappeared, but a new mission formed.

Mission #733: Who was the hottie with the hip-hugging jeans showcasing a heart-shaped ass? Reid would probably know. He knew everyone in town, even most strangers.

"Hubba hubba," Kyle said, followed by a low whistle. "And just who is that delectable creature?"

Reid smirked. "The woman you are admiring, dumbass, is the one you're about to say no to."

No? Why would I say—

Oh. *Oh.* Damn. Bloody Reid. Well, if he thought a cute face—and hot bod—would change Kyle's mind, he was wrong. He would resist her allure. Tell her a firm, yet not too stern, no. Then he would find a way to get her to go out with him, because she was seriously hot.

"Crystal." Reid waved her over, and the goddess with striated brown and blonde hair, an amazing rack—not the pointy kind but the pillowy ones—and creamy skin came over to them.

"Alpha," she said softly.

"Like I've said before, we don't stand on strict ceremony in my clan. Call me Reid. You've already had the misfortune of meeting Travis." The young grizzly grinned at her and winked—which made Kyle's inner beast growl.

Growl? Since when did his caribou know how to growl or show signs of jealousy? Yes, the broad was hot, but still, he'd yet to even talk to her.

Put up your rack, we're not charging anyone, he admonished his animal.

Reid swept his arm past Travis to Kyle. "And this is the guy I was telling you about. Our one and only caribou."

How her green eyes lit at the announcement, and the smile that curved her lips tempted Kyle to the point he missed part of the conversation, his blood-deprived brain tuning in only at the words, "…so glad you're volunteering to help."

"Whoa." Kyle held his hands in a stopping gesture. "About the whole reindeer thing…"

Reid snickered. "And this is my cue to leave. Come on, Trav." With Travis miming gestures of throat slashing and silent, eye-crossing death throes behind Crystal's back, a chuckling Reid and the cub with a death wish, walked away, leaving Kyle alone with Crystal.

She gushed. "I'm sorry, was I babbling? I didn't mean to. I'm just so nervous. After the kindness Reid and everyone has shown bringing me into the clan, I'm determined to give something back and making this parade a success. Something everyone can enjoy. It's so kind of you to volunteer."

"About the parade and stuff, see it was Reid who kind of volunteered me to play a reindeer."

"He did. Thank you so much."

Ouch, talk about having to carefully extricate his tines from the thorny bush Reid had rammed them in. Kyle almost winced as he spoke the next words. "Yeah, don't thank me yet because I'm going to have to decline."

Super happy face, meet utterly disappointed one. The light in her eyes died, and her smile disappeared. "What do you mean decline?"

"See, I've got a certain reputation to uphold, and playing the part of a reindeer clashes with that. I'm sure you understand."

"Sure I do. You're vain." And yes, she dared give him a condescending smirk.

Seriously? He'd killed men for smaller insults. But she was a woman. Sigh. That meant no punching, but more talking. Maybe if he explained? "I'm not vain. I just don't want people to make fun of me."

"Because you're vain. Got some peacock in your lineage?" She mocked him so sweetly it took a moment to grasp her insult.

"Hey. That's not nice."

"Neither is your stupid reason for not helping out in the parade. Then again, I should have expected it from your type." Again with the disparaging tone.

"My type?" His brows rose. "Exactly what type is that?"

"A full-of-yourself jerk. I know all about guys like you. All tattooed up and with your muscles thinking you're the hottest thing on two legs."

Four as well, but he didn't say it.

"You're used to getting what you want with a smile and not giving a hoot about who you might hurt in the process."

"Um, is it me, or are we talking about more than just me here?" Someone had deep-seated man issues.

"None of your business. I'd say it was a pleasure meeting you, but that would be a lie. Thanks for nothing."

With that pert verbal slam, she turned on a heel and stalked away, sweet ass swinging.

I think I might have ruined my chances of getting into those pants.

For some reason, it bothered him more than he would have thought.

Chapter Two

Of all the egotistical things! Crystal couldn't believe the nerve of the man, refusing to participate in a parade because he thought playing the part of Rudolph was beneath him.

What kind of jerk said that?

Kyle did. Stupid, arrogant, good-looking, built-like-a-god, jerk.

It just went to show that where her mandar was concerned she still needed a slap. Hadn't she learned her lesson where good-looking guys were concerned? The only thing they cared about was themselves. They didn't give a damn if dozens of children would end up disappointed. They didn't consider the fact any mirth aimed their way would be the good-natured kind. They just couldn't handle anything they considered a blow to their pride.

A shame because had Kyle shown himself to be a different kind of guy, she just might have enjoyed some blowing—the hot kind, that came from breathless kisses.

There was no denying that despite his vain nature, the man oozed with sex appeal. Totally got her motor running. Probably knew his way around a woman's body. Which meant, he was so wrong for her.

She'd come to Kodiak Point to escape one psycho ex—whom she'd dated for much too long because she thought with her libido instead of her head.

I can't do that again.

Not when it had ended so badly for her and her young daughter.

Poor Gigi. She still hadn't quite recovered from the nastiness of their break up. It was only the mention of the parade, which culminated in Santa being drawn down the main street of town with his eight reindeer, *"And Rudolph!"* Gigi exclaimed, that brought some of the sparkle back to her eyes.

A sparkle Crystal would do anything to have back on a regular basis.

Surely there had to be a way, even on short notice, to find something or someone that could play the part?

Alas, when she'd approached Reid after she was notified they'd lost the reindeer who would have counted as Rudolph, the only person Reid could think of who could even remotely pull off the role was Kyle.

And he'd made his position clear. *Too good to be a reindeer indeed.* If she ever caught his caribou ass out in the wild, maybe she'd let her cougar play with him a while. A few scratches might not change his mind, but it would make her feel better.

But not as good as I'd feel if I was scratching his naked back in my human skin.

Sigh.

"What wrong, Mama?" Gigi startled her with the question, and it took Crystal a moment to spot her child among the parade paraphernalia scattered throughout the large hangar-like garage. The massive space appeared as if Christmas had puked on it. Everywhere she looked, there were mounds of stuff. Boxes overflowing with tinsel, trailers pre-decorated with Christmas scenes and lights on sledge runners for easy movement along the packed snow and ice on the roads. Amongst the structures and chaos, hung costumes, a veritable army of elves, snowmen, and abominable snow beasts.

Gigi's little face peered at her from between a pair of red-striped thermal leggings.

Crystal dropped to her knees. "Munchkin, what are you doing hiding in there? I thought you were playing with the other children in the recreation room."

"I was."

"And?"

Gigi shrugged, her gaze dropping.

Even though she didn't reply, Crystal could guess. Someone had frightened her. Probably not on purpose. Something as simple as an exuberant father picking up his child and swinging them in the air could have sent her little one scurrying.

Thanks a lot, Malcolm.

"You know no one will hurt you here, right?"

A small nod.

"If anyone ever scares you, just let Mommy know or, if I'm not there, tell Reid, our alpha. He doesn't let bullies hurt little girls. He'll take care of whoever is frightening you." If Crystal didn't rip the face off them first.

"But he's scary too," Gigi confided.

"Because he's alpha. But I promise you, he's only a bear with the bad guys. Not cute little girls."

"Promise?"

"Cross my heart." But she didn't add the die part. No use in tempting the sadistic fates, not when her phone vibrated yet again in her pocket. Message three hundred and two? Three? It didn't matter. Crystal could already guess what it said.

I will find you, and when I do, you'll get your ass back home where you belong.

Someone hadn't taken the news of their breakup well. More like he refused to accept Crystal didn't want to stay with him. She'd changed her number three times now and given it out only to her sister, who lived a few thousand kilometers away, and her grandmother. The asshole didn't care he scared her old Granny out of her wits. He wouldn't let go and cajoled poor Granny into giving the numbers each time. So Crystal kept the current number to stop his harassment, kept it even if he called it constantly. She never answered. Didn't listen to his voicemails. Deleted his texts. It didn't stop his determination to get her back.

It must have driven him nuts when he realized she'd moved again. She already knew Malcolm was pissed he didn't have a clue as to her location. After the last time he found her—only with the overeager aid of a pair of women, armed with pepper spray, did Crystal manage to flee from him. After that, given she had Gigi's safety to think of, Crystal didn't dare tell even her closest family where she'd fled.

Good luck finding me now.

Crystal had found refuge in the most remote location she dared. Kodiak Point. Population of a few hundred led, if accounts could be believed, by an honorable alpha who, when he heard the tale of her plight, welcomed her with open arms and a promise of safety.

In time, Gigi would hopefully believe in that safety and once again become the little girl who used to laugh and smile at the world.

Holding out her arms, Crystal gave her daughter a beckoning nod. Gigi emerged from her hiding spot and nestled in her embrace.

Crystal carried her daughter, first to the community center area where they'd piled their outdoor gear, then to her car to take them to the home they'd made for themselves.

As Crystal buckled her in to her booster seat, Gigi softly said, "Only four more sleepies, Mama, until the parade."

"Just a little excited are we about seeing Santa?"

"And Rudolph."

And Rudolph. Dammit. Crystal couldn't help thinking of Kyle and finding herself riled all over again.

Was it too much to ask that her daughter get the one thing she wanted this Christmas? A chance to see Rudolph guide Santa's sleigh.

Yet one man would ruin her daughter's simple dream.

Grrrr.

Or maybe not.

Crystal hadn't missed the way Kyle had initially eyed her. She knew that look. Recognized that smoldering interest.

If it took playing dirty to get her daughter what she wanted for Christmas…well then, dirty she'd play. Time to get out the good bra—the one that pushed her breasts together to form some serious cleavage—and her lowest cut, form-fitting sweater and put her boobs to work convincing a certain vain caribou he wanted to play the part.

Chapter Three

The next day, Kyle took the day off work. Being an electronics specialist for the clan meant he kept busy. There were always things needing fixing, from surveillance cameras to computer networks to helping Reid program his latest phone—because a certain alpha had a tendency of pitching his at the wall when he didn't like the news. While not a computer programmer, he did have a knack for wiring—and loved to make things go boom. A skill he didn't have much use for now that he'd retired from the military.

Except for holidays. He put together some kick ass light displays.

Today, however, Kyle intended to perform work of a different kind. He took himself bright and early to the parade headquarters. Not because he'd changed his mind. No way was he playing Rudolph. However, given he was a master of all things electrical, he thought he could perhaps redeem himself by volunteering to help with lights and sound effects.

Sounded altruistic. Problem was, Kyle knew the real reason he arrived at the community center bright and early—and, yes, eleven o'clock was early for his ass to get moving. But he managed it, with a few cups of coffee. After all, he wanted to impress a certain cougar.

Since he'd met Crystal the night before, she'd not left his mind—at all. Ever heard that expression, 'Hey, baby, you must be tired because you've been running in my mind all night'? Yeah that totally applied to him. Kind of baffling really. Kyle usually didn't give women who exited his line of sight much of a second thought. Usually. Yet not this time.

She'd completely dissed him. Shown him no respect, not an ounce of interest. And yet…

I have to see her again.

Something about the cougar—her scent, appearance, hell, even her attitude—drew him.

Given he didn't know where she hung out in her free time, or lived, he figured the best way to bump into her again was at parade central, which for those unfamiliar with Kodiak Point meant the community center in the heart of town. Probably the largest building beside Beark Enterprises.

Given shifters needed lots of exercise, especially in the case of the young ones, a safe place to expend energy was needed. Hence the reason the space was truly grand. Boasting an Olympic-sized pool, a few gymnasiums, an indoor running track, as well as a massive community hall—because shifters did so love a good ol' fashioned family reunion or wedding—the place had it all. Along with a massive garage area, which was where the various floats were parked as people worked on them.

Now some folks were probably thinking, small town, rinky-dink floats.

Stop right there. Given winter, especially the time around Christmas, saw the bulk of their day revolve in darkness, keeping busy was paramount. You didn't want to let those pesky doubts wiggle their way in. (Mission #417: Don't let the darkness turn you psychotic.)

To battle dark thoughts, what better way than some friendly rivalry? It was also a chance to show off some creative talent while the shadowy hours ticked away. And there was an element of pride, of course, in presenting the most awesome float around.

Given there were only a few hundred inhabitants, the fact they could boast seventeen floats plus a kick-ass Santa sleigh, was downright incredible.

But a pain in the furry ass to manage.

The problem was a bunch of animals cooped together, competing for title of most wicked float, could result in a zoo-like atmosphere. Or at least it had in previous years. It was a reason why Kyle tended to avoid the place this time of the year, lest he get embroiled in an overzealous feud. Like the year when the snowfoxes had their Winter Wonderland float insulted by the brown bears, whose contribution that year was a giant Christmas dinner display. Ever see a four-foot turkey leg take out a copse of fir trees? It was less traumatizing than watching the snowfox nimbly jump on the swinging Styrofoam thigh and launch itself at the bear's head, who let out a god-awful girly scream—which Buster had yet to live down. It started a fake snow and even faker food fight.

As Kyle glanced around, he was amazed by the fact people seemed to work in harmony. Or at least weren't nagging at each other. Was it Crystal's doing, or had the town gotten infected with a dose of goodwill—in the form of Jackson lacing the Nanaimo bars with pot again? That resulted in a massive shortage of snacks all around town as chips and sugary goods got consumed in ridiculous amounts. It also led to a few bloody battles as people duked it out for the last Oh Henry chocolate bar and the only pint of ice cream left in the frozen aisle at the grocery store.

For those wondering, Kyle won in both cases.

But Kyle didn't really care that, for once, things appeared to run smoothly. Kyle was on a mission; mission #735 to convince a certain cougar to give him a chance. #734? Oh, that one had to do with getting some carrot muffins—a dozen for breakfast and rare this time of the year, given their one jackrabbit family had a tendency of stockpiling—and a frozen banana and strawberry smoothie. Mission accomplished.

Craning his head left then right, Kyle perused the vast room until he spotted her. Just as hot as before. Holding on to a clipboard, intent expression on her face, wearing indecently tight jeans—his favorite kind—and a tight knit shirt molding the most perfect breasts, Crystal didn't immediately notice him.

So he stared at her. Nothing like kicking an animal's instinct into gear. He doubted her cat would let her ignore his determined gaze for long.

Wrong.

She didn't whip around to stare back. He focused harder, studying her every feline move, the way the ponytail tickled the back of her neck. Mmm, that exposed neck was tempting.

While she engaged many people, she never once turned his way. Perhaps her predatory instincts were defective.

Or she doesn't consider you a threat, snorted his beast.

He really needed to work on the mission to improve his reputation. This was unacceptable.

He didn't give up. He stared and stared, ignoring the amused glances of others. He wouldn't let her win. And finally, aha, her gaze strayed his way. He shot her his most engaging grin. It flopped as her eyes swept past him and she pretended not to see him.

He frowned. This was new. Usually when he smiled, people smiled back. Had he lost his touch? Was his smile broken?

Mission #736: Check status of panty-dropping grin.

He directed his best smile at a gaggle of mothers chatting in a group beside a gingerbread house float—made of real gingerbread and candy. Sugar rush heaven for kids and adults alike.

But back to his hundred-watt smile. Eyelashes fluttered, flirty smiles replied, and one even waved at him.

Mission accomplished.

Everything was working fine on his end, so why did Crystal seem immune?

She wandered away from him, and he lost sight of her behind a giant Frosty the Snowman rendition.

After adjusting himself, because a man didn't chase after a woman without first making sure he still owned his balls, he followed.

His excuse: he needed her to assign him a task.

Real reason: *Want to get closer.* A simple need, but a strong one that didn't just have elements of the man demanding it, but his caribou too. It seemed his beast was intrigued by the cougar—a predator of his kind.

I always did like to court danger.

The garage buzzed as various townsfolk worked on the floats. A radio somewhere played Christmas music—a crooning melody that talked about a white Christmas. Never a problem this time of year.

Reaching the big snowman, he turned the corner, only to rein in a scowl of disappointment. Where had she gone to? With all the various scents crowding the place, he couldn't track her, not that his sense of smell was the greatest. That was more of a canine trait.

Tenacious when on a mission, Kyle didn't give up. He wandered around and found himself offering a hand to the folks setting up a manger scene, which for some reason required him to staple some tinsel to a two-by-four. On the Grinch float, he slapped on some duct tape to hold down some wires. He even crawled under a trailer to find a loose connection that, once spliced, caused the lights to erupt in blinding brilliance, which in turn resulted in a small cheer from the group working on it.

During his various tasks, Kyle didn't run into Crystal, but he did catch the occasional glimpse. Problem was, by the time he was done with his latest helpful stint and had moved in her direction, she'd disappeared again.

Damned woman. Can't she stay still for just five minutes?

Nope. And then she utterly disappeared. He scouted the whole room without finding a trace. That was when he should have called it quits. Left. Maybe gone and grabbed a beer and flirted with someone else.

Not this man on a mission.

By damn, he'd shown up at the crack of not even noon to see her, and he would find her. With some help. He stuffed his pride in his pocket, promised it a treat later, and sauntered over, casual like of course, to ask Ursa, Reid's grandmother, if she'd seen the girl.

Her eyes twinkled. "Why, Kyle, don't tell me there's finally a lady who is immune to your considerable charms?"

Yeah, it baffled him too. "We got off on the wrong hoof."

"So I hear. Have you changed your mind about playing the part of Rudolph?"

Kyle almost squirmed under Ursa's intent gaze. He'd served under the toughest rhino around in the military. He could surely withstand the laser-like stare of one old lady. He did—barely. "No."

"A shame."

That was all she said, but Kyle felt rebuked nonetheless. "I'm sure the parade will be fine without Rudolph leading the way."

Ursa made a noise. "If it makes you feel better to think that."

Why did everyone insist on acting like it was such a big deal? So what if he didn't want to play a red-nosed freak? It wasn't as if he was single handedly destroying Christmas. "If we're done with the guilt trip, can you tell me where Crystal is?"

"I thought I saw her heading toward the stable."

The stable with its smelly domestic animals. Ugh. For some reason, Kyle disliked the place. Not because it was dirty or ill-kept. On the contrary, animals cared for by shifters tended to be the most spoiled creatures around.

Still though, the whole locked-in-a-box aspect wigged Kyle out. He'd spent his time in a tiny prison—too much time—and he hated any reminder of it. Thus, Kyle almost decided to wait until she returned. But then, it occurred to him that if she saw him among those simple-minded beasts, she'd perhaps better understand his position. In a comparison between the two, she'd see he just wasn't cut out to be a reindeer.

Since the animal pens weren't too far, he forewent donning a jacket and jogged to the stables. As soon as he entered, the warmth of the place quickly dispelled the chill, and his blood heated as he caught sight of Crystal stroking the nose of one of the creatures.

I've got something you can stroke. Down, boy. Damn, but she had the ability to bring out his randy side. Listening to her didn't improve matters.

"Aren't you a handsome fellow?" she crooned. "Look at you with those big brown eyes and that impressive set of antlers."

Ha. His rack was much larger. Everything about him was large.

"I could just rub you all day."

A spurt of jealousy at the attention the deer was getting made him feel a need to point out, "You know they don't understand you."

"And you don't understand me. It doesn't seem to stop you from wanting to have a conversation because I assume that's why you followed me." She continued to stroke the beast's nose instead of facing him.

It irked him, especially since she'd guessed the reason for his appearance. He didn't admit it though. "What makes you think I followed you?"

She stared at him pointedly with her piercing green eyes, and she arched a single blonde brow.

Okay, perhaps he was a tad obvious. He grinned as he spread his hands in capitulation. "Fine, you caught me. I did follow you out here to talk. I came to apologize for yesterday."

"So you've changed your mind?"

"No. But—"

"There are no buts. Unless you've changed your mind and you're planning to help me with our Rudolph problem, then I have nothing to say to you."

"We don't have to talk. We could just make out." Even for Kyle, it was brazen, and, judging by the wide eyes on Crystal, totally unexpected.

"You did not just say that?" she sputtered after a few moments of stunned silence.

Even though he'd blundered, he forged ahead. "So is that a no?"

"Try never."

"Why not?"

Again, she couldn't help an incredulous expression. "Do you seriously have to ask?"

"Is this only because of the whole Rudolph thing? Because if it is, then it's pretty silly. I mean, seriously, what's the big deal if you don't have a red-nosed guy pulling the sleigh? It's not like it's the end of the world."

"Not to you perhaps," she muttered mysteriously. Clipboard tucked under her arm, she stalked toward him, but when she went to go around his frame, he shot out an arm and blocked her.

"Come on. Give me a chance. I'm really not the jerk you're making me out to be."

"I doubt it."

"Have dinner with me."

"No."

"Why not?"

"Because I don't like you."

"Because you haven't gotten to know me." He gave her his best aw-shucks smile.

Her expression didn't change. "And I don't want to."

"You see, your lips say you don't want to, and yet, your body says otherwise." His eyes perused her, noting the hard tip of her breasts poking her sweater visible through the unzipped vee of her jacket, her heightened heart rate, and the flushed appearance of her cheeks.

"I might not be able to control my hormones, which I'm suspecting more and more are in need of therapy, but my cognitive abilities are working fine. And they're saying walk away."

Which she did, ducking under his arm and exiting through the door, the cold blast of air doing little to relieve the feverish heat in his body.

Damn, but that woman stoked him on so many levels.

He almost chased after, would have except something caught his attention. Something out of place in the stable.

Given the problems their town had recently with attacks and jabs at the inhabitants, Kyle couldn't ignore it.

"Who's there?" Was it someone he needed to possibly silence for having borne witness to his ignoble defeat when it came to snaring a date with the stubborn Crystal?

No one replied, and yet the sense he wasn't alone—and, no, he didn't count the reindeer—wouldn't leave. Someone was in the barn with him.

"Come out, come out, wherever you are," he sang, his hand straying to the holster with the gun he kept strapped under his leather vest.

A rustle in a bale of hay at the far end of the barn snared his attention, and he almost drew his gun, but stayed the motion at the last minute. Good thing, because the head that popped out belonged to a little girl and not the enemy.

Blonde hair in fat curls framing chubby cheeks made the giant green eyes staring at him all the more striking. And freaky. Because she stared. And stared. Yet she didn't say a word.

First impulse? Run from the adorable little girl. Instead, of fleeing from her deadly cuteness, he channeled his sarge and barked, "Who are you? What are you doing here?"

Her eyes widened, and with a squeak of fear, she dove back into the hay.

Brilliant. Just brilliant. He'd scared a little girl. As if he didn't suffer enough guilt, now he felt like a total seal. Which rhymed with heel. But seals were dumber than his foot.

And barking at a tiny little girl definitely ranked as dumb.

I should just walk away before I make things worse. But given her age and the fact there wasn't another adult around…

Sigh. He gentled his tone. "I'm sorry, sweetie. I didn't mean to sound so gruff. You took me by surprise, which, hey, is pretty impressive considering I used to be in the army."

Not a creature stirred, not even a child.

How about a promise? "I won't hurt you."

Nothing.

"Does anyone know you're here?" In other words, was there an adult nearby freeing him to escape this uncomfortable situation?

A slight rustle of hay answered him but didn't clarify the situation.

Another heavy sigh left him. "Come on, sweetie, I can't leave you here alone. Reid would have my a—um, butt. Talk to me."

Slowly, the golden curls emerged with bits of straw stuck to them. Big eyes blinked at him.

"Are you lost? "

She shook her head.

"Does you mom or dad know you're here?"

A negative shake.

"Can I help you?"

She tilted her head and perused him. What was it with certain members of the opposite sex? Where did they learn that ability to give you a look? You know the one. The look that made you want to squirm, knowing you were probably coming up short in their estimation.

Except, he didn't fail this time. As if seeing something that satisfied her, the little blonde cherub nodded before lisping, "Yes."

"What can I help you with, sweetie?"

"Not me. Santa."

A frown creased his brow. "Santa?" He almost said, "You mean Earl?" before it occurred to him the little girl might not yet know that the big, burly geezer was playing the part. She was still of an age where magic seemed possible and big fat guys on sleighs could and would deliver presents.

"I heard you talking. You need to find Rudolph. Santa needs him for his sleigh."

Oh crap on a stick. The little girl had heard him discussing the whole Rudolph thing with Crystal, and she'd drawn her own youthful conclusion. How to explain without revealing anything?

"Sorry, sweetie, I wish I could help." *You could,* chided his conscience. *You're just choosing not to.*

Shut up, he snarled at his own mind. Bad enough when Reid and Crystal guilted him. He didn't need his own thoughts to add to the pile.

How could one pair of eyes look so sad? Ack. Kyle almost made the sign of the cross in front of her because surely she had some kind of magic at work because he almost said the most ridiculous thing. He almost told her not worry, that Rudolph would be there.

Never!

"Why don't you climb out of that pile of hay and come with me? We'll go find your parents. They're probably worried."

She shrank from him.

For some reason, this caused a painful pang in him. She was too young to show such fear. Yet he knew that look. He'd borne it when he was a kid and his father came home in one of his moods. "Oh, sweetie, don't be scared. I won't hurt you."

"But you're big."

"Yes I am. And strong." Hmm, maybe he shouldn't have pointed that out.

She nodded. "You are, and scary," she added.

"Me?" He grabbed at his chest in mock horror. "Is this your way of telling me I'm ugly?"

A small giggle escaped her. "No, silly. But handsome doesn't mean nice. That's what my mama says."

"In some cases, probably, but not this time. Why, I'm the nicest guy you'll ever meet."

"Malcolm said he was nice too, but he wasn't. He was mean to my mama, and me."

Wouldn't Kyle love to teach this *Malcolm* a lesson about treating a woman right? "Well, I'm not this Malcolm guy, and I can tell you right now, I'm never mean to the ladies." Even stubborn ones. "And I'll tell you something else, if that Malcolm dude were to walk in here right now and try anything, I'd totally kick his ass." Whoops on the language.

Thankfully she didn't seem to notice. "You're a knight?"

Almost did he snicker, but she seemed so serious. He held it in. "Knight in tattooed armor, sweetie. So don't you worry that pretty little head of yours. No one will so much as fart in your direction while I'm around."

She giggled. "Farts don't hurt."

"But they sure stink," he said with a smile and a moue of distaste.

Apparently it took a bodily function jest for her to decide he was trustworthy. She emerged from her pile of hay, clutching a ragged stuffed animal in a chubby fist. When he held out his hand, he expected her to clasp it.

Instead, she tucked into his reach and lifted her arms.

Despite him not spending much time around children, Kyle recognized the universal gesture for 'pick me up'. He did, the little girl's weight feather-light even with her jacket and boots.

"Where to, sweetie?"

"Mama's working on the parade for Santa."

"Then let's go find her." Maybe he could also get some clues on this Malcolm fellow, who seemed to think it was cool to threaten women. Kyle wanted to speak with the guy—with his fists.

Mission #737: Find this Malcolm dude and teach him a lesson. A Christmas gift to the little angel in his arms.

Chapter Four

"What do you mean, she's not here?" Crystal almost said again to Abigail, the frazzled woman in charge of the daycare area. It took a ton of patience to volunteer to help wrangle very active children, especially shifter ones who had an abundance of energy, and an agility that saw them climbing everything in sight. Still though, her understanding only went so far. Crystal could have shaken the woman when she returned to grab Gigi only to realize she was missing.

It wasn't really their fault. Gigi was a master when it came to escaping places, especially daycares. Problem was, where did she go?

People milled about everywhere. There were hundreds of places a little girl her size could hide.

But Crystal would find her. She always did. *Thank you, Malcolm* for being such an asshole.

Given his outbursts, which they could never predict, poor Gigi had developed a habit of hiding herself when she got frightened. Thing was, it didn't take much. Any kind of raised voice. A male with a loud laugh. Even the most mundane thing could send her daughter scampering.

In time, Crystal hoped that as life returned to normal—and prove safe—in Kodiak Point, that Gigi would lose the defensive habit and would find some measure of confidence.

She started her search in the community center, but it didn't take her and her refined sense of smell long to realize that her daughter wasn't amongst the screaming and yelling kids.

And, her coat was missing.

I'll bet she's back among the floats. Her daughter had a fascination with them, and it seemed every time she pulled a Houdini, the hectic place with all the trailers and glitters was where she hid.

Starting at one end of the garage, Crystal began her search, only to stop not long after as her daughter turned up in the most unexpected spot. Kyle's arms.

Surely a hallucination.

She rubbed her eyes and pinched herself before looking again.

The situation hadn't changed. Her shy daughter clung to Kyle, perched on his burly, tattooed arm, looking for all the world as if she belonged there. And was she actually smiling?

Blink. Still the same. Crystal almost asked someone to slap her. *I'm mistaken, or it's the glare from the lights.* Gigi rarely smiled, and she certainly never let strange men touch her or carry her around or anything.

When several moments went by and nothing dispelled the mirage, Crystal began to believe it, but still didn't understand it. How, and when, had Kyle gained her daughter's trust?

He probably cheated and used that hundred-watt smile.

The jerk.

The night before, Crystal might have gone home with a plan of attack, determined to use her feminine wiles to seduce the caribou into capitulating. Her determination didn't last. By morning, her belly was streaked with yellow.

Given her recent experience with Malcolm, Crystal was still gun-shy. Or was it man-shy? Either way, getting involved, even if briefly or flirtatiously, with a man like Kyle—vain and thinking himself God's gift to women—wasn't healthy for her. Fun probably, exciting in the bedroom, but in the long run, any kind of dalliance would just hurt Crystal, and possibly Gigi.

When it came to dating and men, Crystal needed to pay more attention, to not let herself get caught up in the packaging and really examine what was inside a guy. In retrospect, she should have noted the signs with Malcolm, but as a single mom working two jobs trying to support her daughter—because of a deadbeat father who took off to parts unknown when he found out—she craved attention, someone to love her.

Malcolm saw her weakness and exploited it. He put on such a good act. Convinced her he loved her, told her they could be a family, that he'd take care of her.

He did. Just not in a way any woman would find healthy.

However, she'd escaped the prick. Her life with him belonged in the past. She now lived for the future, a future where Gigi and Crystal would come first.

They didn't need no stinking man to complete them.

They didn't need a good-looking guy with a brilliant white smile.

Or giant muscles.

Or an infectious laugh.

Time to snare her daughter back before Crystal made any other disturbing discoveries. *Such as whether or not he kisses with his eyes open or shut.*

Off she marched, libido firmly leashed, pacing cougar caged in her mind.

Gigi noted her first and waved before palming Kyle's cheeks and lisping, "My mama is coming."

Well, at least she couldn't accuse him of trying to use her daughter. Genuine surprise creased his face as he beheld her, the slack-jawed, eyes-wide-open type.

"Crystal is your mother?"

Blonde curls bobbed.

"Figures," he muttered.

"Hey, little Houdini, where were you hiding this time?"

"In the stable."

Where Crystal had just been but failed to note her own daughter's presence. Some hunter/tracker she'd make. *Goodbye Mother of the Year award too.*

She held out her arms, yet Gigi held back. What the hell?

Instead, Gigi hugged the big caribou and beamed. "Kyle found me."

Kyle? They were already on a first-name basis. How nice. She reached for her daughter again. "Come on, Gigi. Time to go home and get some supper. You must be hungry."

This time her daughter didn't hesitate, practically throwing herself at Crystal. She caught the armful with a grunt and a stagger, an unsteady wobble steadied by a hand.

The simple touch shouldn't have sent a jolt of awareness through her, but it did.

No. No. No. Not good. She stepped away from Kyle. "Thanks for finding her."

"You're welcome. She's a great kid."

Ha. Like she'd fall for his compliment. Using Gigi as a ploy to get in her good graces wouldn't work. "The best, and in need of food before she turns into a scratching and spitting hellion. Bye."

Not giving him a chance to reply, she strode away from him with Gigi on her hip, trying to ignore the fact her daughter peeked over her shoulder and waved.

Before they headed outside into the cold, she zipped Gigi's jacket and pulled hats and mitts from her pockets, placing them snugly on her daughter's hands and head.

Then, with Crystal holding Gigi firmly by the hand, they braved the chilly night but not dark, as the community center had lights strung at regular intervals in the parking lot.

Light did her little good though when her car refused to start. It chugged sluggishly, once, twice, three times before it died. Nothing. Zilch, not even a click.

Sitting in the frigid vehicle, she stared at the dash in annoyance. Stupid old piece of junk only started when it felt like it, which was getting less and less often.

It looked like they'd have to walk home, which in good weather was only about fifteen-twenty minutes, but in the sub-zero temperatures, lugging a tired and hungry little girl? Ugh. Taxis weren't exactly common out here. She could probably go back inside, though, and score a ride from someone.

A tap on her window made her squeak.

A familiar visage peered at her. "Need a lift?" Kyle asked.

Pride or convenience?

Minutes later, they'd transferred, Gigi, her booster seat, and Crystal to Kyle's truck. While the warm cabin sure beat an arctic walk, it also made her uncomfortably aware of him. His scent. His maleness. His wicked smile. His conversation with her daughter.

"So, sweetie, whatcha asking Santa for Christmas?"

"I want the Lego Friends Mall."

Which at one hundred and thirty dollars wasn't likely to happen. "Remember what I said, Santa can't always get you exactly what you want." With about fifty-six dollars saved, Crystal could get her daughter a smaller building set and a few items from the Dollar Store, but only if she managed to find a sitter for Gigi and hitch a ride to a bigger town over the next few days, else she'd have to make do with whatever their local shops had in stock.

"I know, Mama. Santa does his best," said Gigi, with all the exasperation a child could manage who'd heard a speech one too many times. "I just hope he can find me without Rudolph to guide his sleigh."

Crystal almost grinned as Kyle stiffened. Nothing like having the cutest little girl on earth inadvertently guilt a man.

It didn't take long for them to reach their home. "This is the place," Crystal announced, and Kyle pulled his truck against a snowbank by the curb.

Home sweet home. Not much, an apartment over a book store that she got rent free in return for working evenings a few nights a week. The owner, an old lady, was friends with the Alpha's grandmother. Between that and the pittance she earned from Reid for managing the parade—which she personally called charity, but he called a business deduction—she was managing to stay afloat, but she'd need a steadier, better paying job if she wanted to get ahead.

"Thanks for the ride." Crystal unbuckled Gigi before sliding out of the passenger side. Standing on the ground, she held out her arms and lowered her daughter before she turned to reach back in for the booster seat.

Kyle's hand stayed hers. "Might as well leave it for the morning."

"Excuse me?"

"Your car's broken, and you'll need a ride. So what time am I picking you up?"

"We usually get there around nine a.m. but—"

"Nine? That's practically the crack of dawn."

"Dawn's currently later than that."

"Still. It's early."

"Then don't come. We'll manage fine on our own."

"No, you won't because I'll be here. At nine." He flashed her a smile as he leaned over to snag the passenger side door. She moved out of the way as he pulled it shut.

Only after he pulled away did she think to say, "Don't bother." But it was too late.

Too late for a few things, such as stopping the hero worship in a certain little girl's eyes. "Isn't Kyle great, Mama? He's a knight."

"Oh really?" She would have termed him more a rake.

"He's going to save me from bad guys."

If only he could, little one. Especially pesky ones, she thought with irritation as her phone vibrated, again, against her hip. "Come on, munchkin, let's feed you before you turn into a dragon he needs to slay." To the sound of her daughter's giggles, they went inside.

The next day Crystal didn't hold out much hope that Kyle would show up at nine. She'd noticed him arriving at parade central a touch before noon the day before with the look of a man who'd recently rolled out of bed.

Alone or not?

None of her business. It didn't stop her from wondering, though.

Just like she wondered why she couldn't stop thinking of him, or noticing his every move. She could have sworn every hair on her body rose the moment he'd entered the stable yesterday. It was one thing to ignore him in a room full of people but almost impossible when alone.

So I'll just make a point of avoiding alone-time with him.

She'd planned to start by getting ready early and avoiding his offer of a ride altogether.

The jerk ruined that plot by showing up at eight, bearing coffee and donuts.

No, not the donuts!

If Gigi was enamored of him before, he now had entered a god-like realm. As her daughter happily licked chocolate icing while watching *Treehouse*, Crystal eyed Kyle over her steaming cup of coffee—three sugars with cream. Just how she liked it.

"This isn't going to work," she said, going on the offensive.

"What won't work?" was his innocent reply.

Innocent? Ha. "This. The coffee, donuts, you being so nice to Gigi."

"First off, I like your daughter, and I liked her before I knew who her mother was. Second, well, I'm guilty of the second part. Once I knew where you lived, it wasn't hard to figure out where you might go for coffee and to bargain that info out of Mario." Mario being the fellow who owned and ran the only coffee shop in town.

"Bargain? What exactly did you promise him?"

"I've got to go over on Boxing Day and hook up his boy's Xbox system that he's getting for Christmas."

She snickered. "I see Mario's a busy fellow. In exchange for coffee and donuts twice a week, I give his mangy cat a bath."

"That beast? You're a brave woman."

"Not really. One good snarl from me and he's putty in my hands."

"Putty, eh? I don't know how soft you'd find me if you got your hands on me." Nothing subtle about his innuendo or grin.

Flustered, because despite her pep talk to herself she was tempted by his charm, Crystal turned to more mundane matters, such as wiping sugar off Gigi's hands and face then bundling her in to her outerwear.

As they drove to the community center, she noted a tow truck by her car.

"Oh no. What's he doing?" she exclaimed.

"Pete's taking it to his garage for a peek. Although, if you ask me, I think you should send it to the scrapyard. That car's done its time."

"I can't afford a new one, just like I can't afford someone to look at it," she muttered, not without some embarrassment.

"Don't worry about the cost. Pete owes me a few favors."

"Favors you should keep. I can't pay you back."

"No one said you had to."

No, but her pride had already accepted too much charity of late. "Why are you determined to help me?"

Gigi, with the simple eloquence of a child, had a quick response. "Because he's a knight, and knights always help princesses in trouble."

Not in Crystal's world. But maybe the cycle would end with her daughter, who seemed to have found a champion in Kyle. Thing was, Crystal knew better than to expect anything for free. Ultimately, he'd expect something in return. Something she bet that would involve tongue and naked skin.

Dream on.

Once they reached the community center, she tried to ditch him with the excuse of bringing Gigi to the daycare area. However, her daughter resisted.

"I don't wanna go." A jutting lower lip completed her stubborn refusal.

"Mama's got a few things to do, and then we can go home." Crystal waited for the second half of their usual argument where she begged to stay with Crystal. A family therapist she'd spoken to had urged Crystal to encourage her daughter to spend time with others to foster independence. Whether Gigi liked it or not, spending time with other children was necessary. So Crystal prepared her rebuttal as her daughter opened her mouth.

"Wanna stay with Kyle."

Rewind. Crystal stared at her daughter. That wasn't part of their usual script.

"Who wants to hang with me?" Kyle asked.

Crystal jumped in before her daughter could. "No one. I'm sure you've got better things to do than have a little girl underfoot."

"I could use an assistant." Kyle crouched and brought himself eye level with Gigi. "What do you say? Want to assist me?"

She nodded eagerly, and Crystal found herself torn. It was a big step for her daughter to show a willingness to spend time with someone other than her mother. But, on the negative side, it was with Kyle. Need she really say more?

Shining green eyes met his, and a chubby hand slid into a large calloused one. Crystal sighed.

Battle lost.

"Let's go spread some Christmas tech help, sidekick," he announced as he swept a giggling Gigi in the air, flying her superman style—with whooshing sound effects.

Talk about playing dirty.

He really was pulling out all the stops in his quest to seduce Crystal. Just how much dirtier could he get? For some reason she couldn't help imagining him stripping, revealing the bod he hid, and stepping into a shower to clean himself, of course, in preparation for the *really* dirty things next on the menu.

Thank goodness he wasn't around to witness her shiver.

What an incredibly dangerous man. So deadly. The more Crystal watched him—wanted him, and yes, fantasized—the more she feared succumbing to his charm.

As for her guileless daughter? Alas, poor Gigi was a goner.

And who could blame her?

Crystal kept a close eye on them, as any mother would with an almost stranger—one with an ulterior motive—who hung around her child. It didn't help her dilemma.

When Gigi accompanied Crystal, she did so with a painful shyness around people. If a cashier addressed her, she ducked behind her mother. She'd stare at her feet instead of replying. If someone spoke too loudly, especially a man, with eyes wide, lip trembling, she'd fly for the comfort of her mother's arms.

Or did, until she wrapped Kyle around her itty-bitty baby finger.

The man, who it seemed was some sort of technical genius when it came to wiring, was in demand as he strolled around, Gigi perched on his shoulders, where, with the pointing of a finger, she directed his movements. When they hit a float in need of a hand, he'd put her daughter down.

It fascinated Crystal to see the quick trust Gigi placed in him. If someone frightened her, Gigi backed into Kyle, and he'd either hug her, whisper something, or place his hand on her shoulder or head, which for some reason eased the visible tension in her daughter.

And when he barked at someone for using a cuss word in front of a little girl, Gigi didn't flinch or cringe. Instead, the minx beamed up at him.

Crystal spent the morning in an odd state of disbelief. *It's like I'm living some really weird Christmas movie. Like* Twilight Zone *meets* Scrooged.

At lunch, they joined up in line to grab a plate of food—mountains of sandwiches, potato salads, and roasted chicken, because shifters could never have too much meat. The community hall buzzed with conversation as folks took a break, enjoying the repast donated and made by town volunteers. There were more people than even Crystal expected, the explanation being that, this close to Christmas, most businesses were winding down.

Laughter abounded along with plans.

"We're going to go skiing in the Rockies for the New Year."

"Got some moonshine ready for drinking and some presents to wrap."

"Wait until Jorge sees what I bought for Christmas. It's baby-making time."

Some plans caught her attention. Crystal tuned in to Kyle and what he was discussing with Frank—the guy in charge of the Three Bears float but, in a twist, presented as the Wise Men.

"I'll run to the next town over and grab some more Christmas lights from their Walmart. It's not as big as the one in the city, but it should have what we need."

Crystal butted in. "You're going shopping?" Suddenly the prospect of getting something cool for Gigi this Christmas became a bit more possible. Much as she hated to ask Kyle a favor, in this case, sacrifices had to be made. She needed a gift.

"Yup. Want to come along?"

Kyle and her, together, in his truck? She opened her mouth to say no when it occurred to her she'd not left Kodiak Point in weeks. A change of scenery sounded like fun. But an almost two-hour road trip with him? Could she handle the temptation? "I shouldn't. There's a ton I need to do around here."

"You're right, there is," Frank interjected, still a part of the conversation. "I know I'm not the only one in need of supplies. It doesn't make sense for us all to go. How about we get the lists together, along with some money, and you go with Kyle to make sure he gets the right stuff?"

How to say no when someone made it her job? She made one last feeble attempt. "But what about Gigi?"

"She can come, of course." Kyle beamed down at her. "What do you say, sweetie? Are you up for a road trip and dinner at McD's?"

Neatly, Kyle boxed her in, making it impossible for her to say no. But at least Gigi would serve as a barrier between them on the ride.

Funny how that didn't really work, given that every time she looked over her daughter's head as they rumbled along the ice- and snow-covered road, she caught his attention. And sparks fairly flew.

When they reached the store, Crystal just about dove out of his truck, craving the cold and fresh air. She also strove for mental clarity. A lost cause.

It being midafternoon and this close to Christmas, the place hummed with activity as lots of people got their last-minute holiday shopping done. Kind of like Crystal, who started out buying the stuff needed for the parade, but once she got it all, she decided it was time to ask for yet another favor. Why not, in for a dime, in for a dollar.

As Gigi oohed and aahed over the brightly lit sample trees, Crystal pulled Kyle aside. "I kind of need a few minutes alone. Would you mind keeping Gigi entertained?"

"Why ask for alone-time when I'm more than willing to help?" His wink brought a blush to her cheek as his implication sank in.

"Not for that, you idiot. To get...you know." She inclined her head at her daughter, who giggled at a fat Santa who kept getting stuck in an inflatable chimney display.

"I know. I just really enjoy it when your eyes flash. The angry kitty look is hot." Completely unrepentant about his answer, Kyle grinned, and though she tried to scowl, heat still warmed her cheeks.

Turning from Crystal, Kyle scooped Gigi into his arms. She let out a happy squeal.

"Hey, sweetie, what do you say you and I go check out the—" He dropped his voice and whispered in her ear. Two pairs of conspiratorial eyes peered Crystal's way, and her heart just about turned into a big pile of goo at their shared giggle. And, yes, Kyle giggled. The big, tattooed, vain, stupid, adorable jerk giggled like a schoolgirl—with a deep voice.

I hate him. Because not only did he make her want to try again at love and a relationship, he had the most scrumptious ass in tight jeans when he walked away.

Wasting no time, Crystal headed for the toy section, only to groan in defeat when she located the practically empty Lego section. December twenty-third and virtually all the shelves were bare. Forget a decent-sized play set. Even if she could have afforded the mall one Gigi wanted, or any of the other mid-sized ones, none were left. Crystal had to content herself with the mini play packs. But she consoled herself with the knowledge that at least Gigi would have something under their mini fir tree—which they'd chopped down themselves and decorated with popcorn, colored macaroni, and a mixture of aluminum and Styrofoam balls. The hand-painted monstrosities were truly a crowning achievement to the ugliest tree ever, but they both loved it.

Hurrying with her purchases, Crystal brought them out to the truck and headed back before texting Kyle to tell him the coast was clear.

Meet you at the front door in just a few minutes, was his reply along with a happy face.

Warm breath coalesced into a fog as Crystal stood outside waiting, but she enjoyed the cold air, knowing all too soon she'd find it too hot again in the truck with Kyle. She blamed hunger as the reason why she craned anxiously for a glimpse of Kyle and Gigi.

What's taking them so long?

There was no mistaking the butterflies in her tummy. The tingle in her body. The anticipation thrumming through her.

Ugh. I'm crushing on the caribou.

So much for a new leaf.

Or should she look at the situation in a different light?

She'd come to Kodiak Point to start fresh. To create a new and better life for herself. Her ban on men wasn't a permanent thing, more of a be-more-careful-who-you-choose.

Except, in this case, she wasn't the one necessarily choosing. Kyle seemed bound and determined to become a part of her life. Unlike previous boyfriends, he didn't pretend interest in Gigi while Crystal was around to make himself appear a good guy. Kyle genuinely liked her daughter—*probably because she is utterly awesome.*

"Well, well, well. I never expected to run into you here."

No. Oh no. Oh fuck no.

Crystal needed only to turn her head slightly to meet the sneer on the handsome face of her ex-boyfriend—and violent stalker—to know the day would not end well. "Malcolm." Nothing else. No hello, no sorry I-didn't-answer-any-of-your-hundreds-of-crazy-texts-and-phonecalls. Perhaps if she played it cool, he'd walk away.

He skipped the amenities too. "What luck running in to you here?"

"How did you find me?"

"I was visiting an old college friend for the holidays. It must have been fate we both ended up here at the same time."

"More like bad luck," she muttered.

Her words didn't go unnoticed and his gaze narrowed. Not a good sign. "We need to go somewhere to talk." His tight grip on her upper arm indicated a probably less-than-pleasant conversation.

She yanked and exclaimed, "Let me go. I'm not going anywhere with you."

"Shut your piehole before you cause a scene."

Cause a scene? Oh, she'd cause a scene all right if it kept her out of this psycho's reach.

But, before she could, a gigantic panda came to her rescue?

Chapter Five

Kyle fought it. He truly did, but the allure of Crystal, and her way-too-cute daughter, shoved him off a cliff, which he might have survived, if not for what waited for him at the bottom. Domestication.

Now don't get him wrong, Kyle had no problem settling down, per se. Eventually. But, at the same time, commitment scared him. Just not for the reason most folks thought.

Everyone in Kodiak Point knew him as the ex-soldier and town heartbreaker. He seduced the ladies but never stayed with them. He made no promises, put down no real roots.

Yet, once upon a time, that hadn't been the case. A long time ago, when a certain boy—with a small fuzzy rack—was in high school, he fell in love with a beautiful girl. And she loved him back.

If perfection had a name, then it was Bethany. Imagine a girl who possessed everything a man could desire— kind, sweet, and with a pair of perky breasts to die for. She became his first real girlfriend. His first love. His fiancée before he went off to war.

He did his best to correspond with her while overseas, but there came a time when that wasn't possible. A time when his only focus had been staying alive, and escaping. Oh the despair of those days when he'd used her face to help him through. But he refused to dredge up that unpleasant part of his past. It was a vile place which he'd come to grips with, shoved in a closet, and thrown a giant lock on. Then he tossed the key.

The time after his incarceration by the enemy was a dark time for him, so when he returned, a little bit older, definitely wiser, could anyone fault a man for needing the embrace of his lover? Instead, he received the rudest awakening.

With the most innocent brown-eyed gaze, Bethany tried to justify her actions. "I wasn't sure you were coming back, Kyle." A feeble explanation he still thought, given she'd answered the door almost nine months pregnant, with another man's child.

Yeah, needless to say, the wedding was called off. Kyle heavily supported the local tavern for a few months and might have gone rabid caribou—goring anyone in sight—if not for Reid. Reid had been the one to talk him out of his despair and request he join the clan in Kodiak Point.

"I need a man I can trust. One who knows his way around technology since I'm a dumbass when it comes to anything electrical."

Reid had offered him a chance. A chance to escape the clan he belonged to, where he never knew when he might glimpse Bethany and the man she chose over him—a regular pack wolf. And a mangy one at that.

Kyle jumped on the opportunity for change, but he didn't jump on the bandwagon of love and commitment after that. He never had an interest because that type of betrayal stuck with a man. Colored his view of women in general. Bethany had broken his trust when it came to the concept of love and commitment.

And then Crystal came along. Crystal with her refusal to give in to his charm. Crystal with her strong attitude, protective mama instincts, and a nice rack made to pillow his head—shirtless of course. Add to that a little girl who thought him a knight—*me a freaking knight*, it still made him chuckle—and he was practically a goner.

Heck, since he'd met the pair, he'd already felt the curse of domestication infecting him, his cussing having gone from hardcore to almost sanitary.

Mission #741: No swearing around little sweetie, which came right after mission #740:

Tell Darren if he leers at Crystal's ass one more time, he's going to need money for a dentist.

No cussing. Getting up early. Now shopping. *How soon before they've got me wearing collared shirts that are tucked in instead of hairband, heavy metal T-shirts? How long until I fall victim to the ugly, knit Christmas sweater geekdom that all the manacled husbands wear this time of year?*

Argh. It almost made a caribou want to shed his human skin and take off running for the wild. The beast maybe wanted to flee the harness, but the man had no interest in running.

Nope, instead, Kyle plunged headlong into trouble by taking the cutest little sweetie shopping, first for a gift for her mother. Nothing like a present to soften a lady's stance. He hoped. The hard part was in selecting a gift.

Having not shopped for anyone in years—he preferred to send his mother cards with cash—he dubiously eyed the item Gigi solemnly insisted Crystal needed. "Are you sure she wants this?" he asked.

She nodded enthusiastically. He grimaced as he grasped the item and put it in the cart. He trusted Gigi's judgment. What the heck did he know about gift buying? But just in case Gigi was wrong, he threw in a second present.

Mission #742 accomplished—buy Crystal a gift—it was time for super-secret mission #739. Having spotted Crystal's head in line at the cash registers, he hightailed it with Gigi—seated in the shopping cart, holding on to the handle, giggling as he raced the cart—to the toy section in search of the coolest stuffed toy ever.

Little girl laughter? Coolest sound ever. A man would do anything to cause it.

Mission #743: Have Gigi repeat laughter as often as possible.

Given his newest mission, he had an excuse as to why he was lugging a giant panda bear when he came across Crystal, trying to disentangle herself from the vise-like grip of some guy. *Say it like it is, a dead fucking asshole if he doesn't get his hands off my woman.*

He glared. It had no effect. Then again, nothing screamed I'm-a-tough-guy-who-is-going-to-kick-your-ass-if-you-don't-step-away-from-the-cougar than a big, fluffy stuffed animal. No wonder the guy laughed when Kyle growled, "Be a smart doggy and walk away from the woman." *Mine.*

"Is a guy with a giant teddy bear really trying to threaten me?" Said with utmost disdain and totally unacceptable.

Shaking with fear, Gigi huddled beside the panda Kyle set down. She raised big eyes his way, and he didn't need her softly lisped, "That's Malcolm," to guess the jerk's identity.

Early Christmas present for me. I knew I was a good boy this year. "Threat? I didn't hear a threat. I heard a promise. And this is your last warning. Remove your hands from Crystal or else."

"Or else what, tough guy?"

About to show him what, Kyle had to force his arm to stay at his side as Crystal shook Malcolm's hand free and stepped between them.

A pair of pleading eyes met his. "Kyle, would you please take my daughter and go somewhere while I deal with this?"

As if he'd walk away.

This man is a threat.

Not just to Crystal but to his overall missions in regards to Gigi and Crystal. He'd made promises, and he intended to keep them, not to mention his new knightly reputation required upkeep. Yes, he'd admit, just not aloud, that the idea of being someone's hero appealed. *I would totally rock a leather hero outfit.*

"I'm not leaving," he stated, but he did need Crystal out of the way. Since he doubted she'd move her sweet ass to give him a direct line of sight, he did the most expedient thing. He snaked an arm around her waist and gave a contented grumble when she squealed very feminine-like, and he inwardly exulted at the fact he'd touched her. As suspected, she felt just right.

He set her to his side where she clamped her lips and eyed him with a touch of ire. Gigi threw her arms around her mother, her fright obvious. Crystal ducked down to gather Gigi against her.

My little sweetie scared? No way. Not happening. He'd initially planned to tell Crystal to take Gigi somewhere else while he *spoke* to Malcolm. That changed at her shaking little frame. Someone needed to see that her knight wouldn't let the mean dragon threaten her anymore.

Kyle dropped his gaze to meet the little girl's and asked, "Nose, gut, or jaw?"

Startled, it took Gigi a moment to reply softly. "Nose."

"Nice choice," he replied.

He spun and jabbed so quickly the moron didn't have time to react. Which really was surprising given his wolf genes, which Kyle smelled as soon as he got close.

Pretty packaging with nothing to back it up. As cartilage crunched under his blow, the idiot who should have listened reeled with a holler. Most men at this point would have probably come to the conclusion they were possibly in trouble and that perhaps the smart thing would involve walking away. Or, in this case, running.

Lucky for Kyle, Malcolm the idiot—who had obviously been dropped way more times on his head than anyone Kyle had ever met—still didn't get it. "You fucking asshole! I'll teach you to fucking hit me."

Did the man not realize there were ladies around? "Watch your language," Kyle admonished. "There's women and children around here." The irony of it almost made him chuckle, but he did smile as the idiot gave him the perfect excuse to act—as if Kyle really needed one. The fact the wolf even breathed the same air offended him.

"Fuck—"

Whatever else Malcolm meant to say got lost as Kyle stepped into Malcolm's personal space and kneed him in the stomach. Air whooshed out of the man and bent him double.

Kyle wasn't done, however. He grabbed the man by the hair and walked him away from the girls. While he wouldn't cuss in front of the ladies, there were times when a man needed strong language, times like now. "Listen here, you bloody miserable excuse for a fucking shifter. I'm only going to say this once. Stay away from Crystal and Gigi. If you even so much as think of coming near her, or calling her, or, hell, if you even think of her, I'm going to hunt your mangy ass down and kill you." And enjoy it. It seemed where his ladies were concerned he possessed a bit of a protective streak.

"You wouldn't fucking dare. The law—"

"Can kiss my hairy caribou ass. I know how to make a man disappear and cover my tracks, so trust me when I say, if I want you dead, I'll kill you, and there isn't a fucking law agency in this world that will ever charge me for it. Do you understand me?" Kyle told the idiot this as clearly as he could. Really, he was being super nice, so nice his buddies would have mocked him. But...

Malcolm yelled, loud enough for a little girl to hear, "Fuck—"

Jab to the already broken nose. Another to split a lip. A few more just because it was fun, and then he tossed Malcolm to the ground.

Kyle sighed as he stared at the groaning heap on the ground. "What did I tell you about the profanity? Some people never learn. Remember what I said. Because, next time, I won't be so nice." Look at him, giving this douchebag the Christmas present of being able to crawl away instead of requiring a stretcher.

Kyle turned his back and strode away, not bothering to look around to see if anyone had witnessed the incident.

Would someone call the cops? Maybe, but more likely they'd chalk it up to what it was, a personal matter that needed resolving. Up here in the still-in-some-ways-untamed North, things weren't always done by the letter of the law. Sometimes things were handled a little more directly, a little more violently. It was the shifter way.

At least for those with the balls—or rack—to do it.

Seeing him approach, Gigi squirmed in her mother's embrace until Crystal put her down. The little girl flew at him, arms spread, and he scooped her into his grip. Already, her weight settled on his hip with an odd familiarity.

She tucked her head just under his chin and whispered, "You did it."

"I did. I slayed the wolf."

"Or pissed it off," Crystal muttered as he reached her.

"He won't be bothering you or Gigi again." Because if he did… "Let's go get some dinner. I don't know about you girls, but lugging around that giant bear has given me an appetite." With Gigi on his hip and Crystal lugging his purchase, they made their way to his vehicle.

"Do I dare ask why you have a giant panda?" Crystal asked as she buckled herself into the passenger seat of his truck.

"It's for a special kid I know. Sweetie here helped me pick it."

And that was all he would say on the matter. His enigmatic smile and wink made Crystal purse her lips, but his curious cat held her tongue. A shame. He had so many uses for it.

It took only a few minutes to find some golden arches. Nothing was said of the incident with Malcolm during a dinner of one cheeseburger meal for a kid, a chicken sandwich for a cougar, and several salads for him.

"No meat?" Crystal asked while devouring her burger, a teasing glint in her eye.

"I'm a vegetarian."

She just about choked. "For real?"

"I fail to see the humor."

"So you eat lettuce like a rabbit?" Gigi asked with a guile only children could achieve.

He scowled at them, but they just laughed as he crunched on his salad. Unlike his army brothers, he couldn't take them to the ground, pin their face in the dirt, and rub it until they renounced their carnivore ways.

So he bore it.

Even with their teasing, he'd never felt more content. As they drove back to Kodiak Point, giant panda secured in the back under a tarp, Gigi fell asleep in her booster, her tiny head nestled against Crystal's shoulder.

Given the darkness and the fact they still had a short ways to go before hitting her house, he asked Crystal, "So, this Malcolm fellow, he's an ex-boyfriend?"

"Ex control freak. Current pain. But one I can handle. You didn't have to do that."

"Yes I did. And just so you know, I didn't do it for you."

"Let me guess, it was a guy, my-dick-is-bigger-than-yours, thing."

"First off, never doubt mine is always the biggest. Second, it had nothing to do with you, smartass. I did it for her." He inclined his head Gigi's way. "She needed to see that a guy like Malcolm could be taken down. To see bullies don't always win." That knights existed. But that part he kept to himself.

"In that case, thank you. It's nice to have someone in our corner. Gigi could use it."

He went straight to the heart of his curiosity. "What happened to her dad?"

Crystal shrugged. "Who knows? He found out I was pregnant at nineteen and flew the coop."

"Coward." Kyle spoke without thinking.

"Yeah. He was. He's never seen her. Never contacted me. Nothing."

"I'd never do that." Why he felt a need to state this, he couldn't have said. "A man has a responsibility to his family. His mate. His child." If Kyle ever allowed himself to get domesticated, while he might balk as the halter was placed over his head, once reined in, he would never walk away.

"You might think that, but Cory didn't. We were young. Stupid."

"Were you married?"

She shook her head. "We were never mates, lovers at best. But we had nothing truly in common. We rarely spoke much. Unless it was to ask your place or mine."

A woman who wasn't afraid to admit she had a lusty appetite. While jealousy growled—and scuffed a hoof—he could corral it with the knowledge she was currently single. Not for long, though, if he had a say. "Sounds like he wasn't the right guy."

"Nope. When it comes to men, I've made some bad choices. But at least one perfect thing came out of it." No doubting what she meant, as Crystal leaned her head to touch Gigi's slumbering one.

"Talking about bad choices, I'm going to guess we're grouping this Malcolm dude in that category of mistakes."

"He's in a category all his own," she muttered darkly.

It didn't take a genius to deduce, "You came to Kodiak Point to escape that jerk."

"Escape. Hide. Find protection. As you might have noticed, Malcolm's a tad forceful when he doesn't get his way. Just breaking up with him wasn't adequate. I came here to start over. To show Gigi a different life, a better one, where she doesn't have to worry about the bark of an insecure prick. Where she can still dream and believe in the impossible."

The way she said the last part struck him. "Is this why you're so hell bent on this parade?"

"You could say so. With everything that's happened, I just wanted her to have the perfect Christmas." Crystal grimaced. "I don't know how well I'm doing, though. I can't even get her what she really wants."

"So she doesn't get the exact thing she asked for. If you ask me, you're doing great." And then he did something insane. It was probably a mental lapse, a result of his messed-up past. Whatever the reason, Kyle committed himself with his word, which—sob—was not something he ever broke. "I'll do it."

"Do what?" she asked, her brow creased in puzzlement.

He could still back out. She hadn't guessed. Or he could do the right thing—choke—and throw himself on the grenade of mockery. "I'll be a bloody reindeer." Argh. The horror.

Her lips quirked. "You'll let me harness you with leather straps?"

And tie me to a bed. He nodded.

"You'll wear tinsel in your antlers?"

If he could kill anyone who dared to make fun of him. Again, with a head tilt.

"And the red flashing nose?"

"Do I have to wear the nose?" he complained.

The impish grin on her lips and the sparkle in her eyes? Yeah. He'd have worn flashing lights on any body part she wanted for it.

"The nose is mandatory."

"You're devious," he grumbled.

To that she just laughed, a husky sound that shouldn't have done anything, yet made the hairs on his arms rise as if electrically charged and his cock swell. What a sweet, fucking sound.

A while later, the conversation having made the miles fly by, they arrived at her place. She slid from her side of the truck and went to retrieve her bag from his utility trunk in the back. The tarp with its lump caught her eye. Someone was going to smile when they got that giant panda on Christmas morning.

He met her by the passenger side door, Gigi cradled in his arms.

"I'll take her," Crystal said after she opened the outside door to her apartment that displayed an impressive set of stairs leading upwards to her place.

"I got her. You go ahead and open the door." Yeah, go ahead, so he could admire the flex of her ass as she climbed the stairs. Mission #738: Check out her ass – accomplished.

A small landing at the top meant he crowded her space as Crystal fitted her key in the lock. Opening the door, she stepped in and dropped her stuff on a battered table just inside.

Turning around right after, she reached out her arms for her daughter, and he shook his head. Using the toe of a boot to hold the heel of the other, he slid off his footwear and padded in. Even the toughest male shifters knew not to wear snowy footwear in the house.

"Stubborn man."

He just smiled.

With a shake of her head, Crystal led him into her home, not a big place by any means, but comfortable with the afghan-covered plaid sofa, the fuzzy velvet chair, and the much-too-tiny television.

Really, who could live with anything smaller than sixty inches? And what was this? No game system! Not even a Wii? Unacceptable. He'd have to rectify that.

Funny how he already thought in terms of the future. The domestic collar drew tighter. But he wasn't choking—yet.

There was a narrow hall off the living room with a few doors. One with a wooden carved G led to a small room, and he meant small, with a single bed covered in a bright flowered comforter. Kyle placed the sleeping little girl atop it and then stepped back as

Crystal did her mommy thing, stripping off boots, coat. She handed them to Kyle, who then took them out to the main room and hung them. Then he waited.

A few minutes later, Crystal emerged, but she didn't shut the bedroom door. Instead, she crooked a finger at him. "Gigi wants you."

Me? Puzzled, he went back in, brushing by Crystal as he did, the sweet scent of her wrapping around him all too pleasantly.

Inside the claustrophobic room, a heavy-lidded Gigi smiled at him. She held her arms out as she said, "Night."

He knelt, controlling a need to crush the little body tight to him. The most protective feeling came over him.

Mission #744: Make bedtime tuck-ins a priority for hugs.

By the time Gigi released him, her eyes were already shut, her breathing evening out. He stood and caught Crystal staring at them, sadness hinting her gaze. She turned and padded away. He followed, closing the door softly behind him.

Entering the compact living room, Crystal stood by the most pathetic, yet obviously loved, excuse for a Christmas tree. She fingered a lumpy foil ball on it.

"Thanks again for everything."

"You're welcome."

"I, um, guess, I'll see you tomorrow."

They would. And the day after.

But he wasn't leaving without accomplishing one mission. A new mission.

Mission #745: Kiss the girl.

He took a step toward her. She didn't move, but she eyed him. He took another, stalking her like a predator with a skittish prey, ironic given their opposite roles in the animal kingdom.

When he stood within her space, Crystal having held her ground, she peered at him and licked her lips. She might have even trembled. "I know what you're planning to do."

"I should hope so since it's pretty freaking obvious."

"I can't afford to make another mistake."

A part of him yearned to tell her he wouldn't let her down. He wouldn't screw her over. He would never hurt her like the men in her past. *You can trust me.*

But Kyle was a man who'd just agreed to play the part of Rudolph. He'd already lost enough manly pride for one day. So, instead, he showed his lady what he felt.

Hopefully, she knew how to read tongue.

Chapter Six

He's going to kiss me.

Crystal knew it. Could see it in Kyle's eyes and how he moved toward her, his every motion graceful, powerful, and alert. She wouldn't escape his kiss. Didn't want to.

Call her foolish, but ever since the moment Kyle had stepped up for them, acted the hero Gigi claimed him to be, Crystal had wanted to play the part of damsel. How unlike her to want a fairytale. She'd long ago given up hope on achieving a happily ever after. However, Kyle made her want to believe again. Like when he played the part of knight. A man with valor who still believed in protecting the innocent. A true prince.

Speaking of whom, in all the stories, didn't the guy who saved the princess get a kiss for his efforts?

She should and almost had. Despite her anger that he'd butted in, she couldn't help the elation as he vanquished her daughter's fear by playing the hero and getting rid of Malcolm. In her relief, and yes, pleasure at his actions, she'd almost given Kyle a kiss back in the parking lot at Walmart. As if she needed a reason to smooch those delectable lips of his.

But she did need courage.

Her yellow belly reappeared and kept her from flinging herself in his arms, with valid reason. First off, Gigi was with them, and Crystal preferred to not indulge in that type of activity in front of her daughter. Secondly, she was scared.

Scared she would, once again, make the wrong choice.

What to do? Take a chance, or keep him at arm's length?

For once, it wasn't just her hormones encouraging her to give this guy a chance. After spending time with him, talking with him, and seeing how he was with Gigi, her gut heartily approved. Hell, even her cat purred when he was around. That had never happened before. Was it a sign?

What if I'm mistaken? Could she handle more disappointment? The better question was, would she let fear dictate her choices forever?

Already, she'd spent a year living in limbo, ignoring her needs because of uncertainty and also to ensure Gigi didn't suffer any more disruption. But was exploring the possibilities with Kyle truly that selfish? In finding the right man, a good man, wouldn't that benefit them both?

Surely, at one point, we're due for a run of security and happiness.

Was Kyle the man to help them both? The one who would help them form a family? To help them find a happily ever after?

Gigi certainly seemed to think so. Crystal wasn't blind. She saw the adoration in her daughter's eyes when she looked upon Kyle and noted the trust she placed in him. The difference between the bond Kyle had already formed with Gigi versus the one that had never existed between her daughter and Malcolm seemed so obvious. If Crystal did take the next step, she already knew things would be different.

If Kyle could commit.

He'd already proven the tough guy exterior had a chink. He might have started out thinking he was Joe Cool, but since their introduction, he seemed to have since adjusted his mindset.

Forget the Borg and their assimilation, I am mommy, and I am offering him domestication.

And he didn't seem to mind. It seemed the more time he spent with them, the more he leaned towards a family life that included them. The more she discovered about him, the deeper she sank.

Oh god, I'm falling for him. The revelation stunned her but also vanquished her remaining fear, which was why, when he moved in close, she held her ground, angled her head, and closed her eyes as he swept in for a kiss.

Oh my.

It took only one electrifying press of his lips.

Instant awareness shot through her, a thrill like she hadn't felt since her first kiss. Except there was nothing to stop this embrace. No reason to cease the sensual slide of lips against lips.

Hot breaths merged as mouths parted to allow their tongues to engage in a sinuous dance. Her arms twined around his neck, and his wrapped around her torso, pinning them tight together, tight enough that she could feel the steady pulsation of his heart, the hardness of his body, and the evidence of his erection. There was no doubting his desire, their desire. Their passion…

She raked her fingers through his hair, scratching and tugging, her breath a hot pant, which he inhaled. He hoisted her so she leaned against the wall, his strength a part of him, effortless and so sexy. With his lower body, he pinned hers, rubbing and holding her in place, leaving his hands free to roam. And roam they did while his mouth plundered hers, drawing an aching desire forth.

Touch me, she wanted to moan, but she was past coherent speech, caught in the sensations of the moment.

But he didn't need telling. His fingers found the edge of her shirt and slid under, the rough tips a gentle abrasion on her skin. Feathering touches tickled a path over her ribcage to her fettered breasts. He didn't let the cotton cup deter him.

Nothing screamed sexy like a plain white athletic bra. It didn't seem to bother him. His thumb stroked over the straining peak, the barrier of fabric a sensual layer that only made the moment he shoved it upward, baring her breast, all the more exciting.

She sucked in a breath as he brushed his calloused finger over her nub. Again and again, he rubbed then pinched, which made her gasp. How could the tease of her nipple bring such erotic pleasure to her sex? Who cared? A shudder went through her as he once again squeezed.

And then he stopped. *No.* If she had the breath, she would have protested out loud.

He shifted her body, pushing her higher on the wall, which meant his lips moved out of reach of her own, but that was only because he apparently had another location he needed to explore.

"Kyle." His name whispered out of her as his hot mouth latched on to her nipple. He sucked and twirled his agile tongue around the tip. Each tug, each suck, sent a jab of heat to her sex.

First one breast then the other. He took his time with each, exploring and teasing them as all the blood in her body boiled, all her nerve endings coiled, and her panties grew wetter and wetter.

His lips finally left both of her peaks, not that it stopped their throbbing. His mouth traced a path down her belly until it reached the button on her pants.

She didn't see how he did it, but somehow he managed to get them undone, parted, and he kissed the top of her mound through her panties—more industrial cotton, which didn't stop his sensual seduction.

Or would it?

When he lowered her, setting her on the floor, she almost cried out, but his lips caught hers. And then she didn't mind because it seemed he had a reason to set her free, namely so he could shimmy her out of her pants and tear her panties from her.

One rip. One sexy rip of fabric to expose her to him.

Utterly sexy.

Bared to his touch, he wasted no time and cupped her. Cupped her moist sex with his hand while he sucked at her tongue.

She almost came.

"I'm going to taste you, Crystal," he murmured against her mouth. "I'm going to lick you until you come."

What sane woman wouldn't react to those words?

Hell, she practically came. She most certainly shivered and shuddered. She cried out and clamped down on her peaking pleasure when he dropped to his knees and nuzzled her. Her sex clenched tight as his hands parted her thighs, and she felt the warm brush of his breath against her throbbing pussy.

At his first lick, she almost collapsed, but his hands caught her, held her, made her submit to the decadent torture of his tongue. Sweet, pleasurable, erotic torture.

It didn't take long. The wet and warm licks and sucks of his mouth teased already throbbing flesh. When he flicked the tip of his tongue against her clit, she was a goner.

Only by biting her lip did she manage to keep herself from crying out. But oh how she longed to shout his name. To scream it to the world.

Wave after wave of pleasure rippled through her as he refused to relent in his sensual enjoyment of her sex.

Finally, she could take no more, and she managed to gasp, "Enough."

With a final kiss on her tender parts, he stood and wrapped his arms around her. He hugged her, and she hugged him back, not a word spoken, just basking in an intimate moment that allowed her to gather her wits.

Now that he'd pleasured her, time to return the gift.

But when she went to slide her hands down his body to his waist, he caught them and brought them to his lips, placing a kiss on each before releasing them.

"I should go now."

It took a moment to process the meaning of his words. "You're leaving?" She couldn't help the incredulity in her tone, especially since she could see the evidence of his need bulging against the crotch of his jeans.

"I told you I was different, and I'm going to prove it to you."

"By not having sex with me?" She couldn't help the puzzlement.

"Exactly. I know things are moving fast between us, which is probably freaking you out. I know it's freaking me out a little. But in a good way," he hastened to reassure. "I'm not leaving because I don't want you because, trust me, I do."

"Says the guy about to walk out the door." She was still processing the odd turn of events.

"Leaving to go home to a cold shower and lonely bed."

"You don't have to do that." *Really, you can stay, here with me.* She held back from begging aloud. What was wrong with her? He was trying to act a gentleman, and here she was, practically forcing him to stay.

"Much as it pains me, I have to go. You need time to adjust to what's happening between us. To understand I'm not going to mistreat you and Gigi. That I'm a man you can count on. So, despite the fact I want to stay in the worst possible way, I'm not. Not until I think I've earned your trust."

Honor? That still existed? "You're nuts."

"Borderline certifiable according to the army shrinks." He grinned. "But, unlike my buddy Boris, I don't have a thing for guns, so they let me go. However, while I might not decorate my home in weapons, I do warn you I am a techno freak. Getting together with me means putting up with wired sound to every room in the place. An alarm system that will know if a fly farts. And losing me a few hours a week to gaming with my buddies online."

"You speak as if you're planning to stick around."

A sensual smile stretched his lips. "You mean you hadn't figured that part out yet?"

Hope blossomed, a warm spot in her chest, which she'd not felt in a long while. "I was afraid to think that far ahead," she admitted. "I've been disappointed a lot in the past."

"And that's going to change. From now on, things will be different. For you and Gigi.

Fuck, I can't believe I'm even thinking this way. A few days ago, before I met you, all I could think of was, well, myself," he said with an unrepentant grin. "But now, I'll be damned if the idea of a *we,* as in family, doesn't have more appeal."

"Maybe you got infected with the Christmas spirit. It might wear off."

"More like I got smacked with it, and no, baby, it ain't wearing off. I've made you my mission."

"Mission?" she said with a laugh, oddly enough not perturbed by the fact that she was having a conversation, wearing only a shirt that barely fell low enough to cover her hips, with a man who'd just made her come. What a sight they must present.

"Yes, mission. I'll warn you right now that, as part of my disorder or, as I like to call it, adorable personality trait, I tend to think of things in terms of missions."

She wrinkled her nose. "Okay, and that means what?"

"Well for example, I'm working on mission #746: Be the best fucking Rudolph ever for one little girl."

How ridiculously disturbing, yet cute. "I like that mission, and do you have any missions concerning me?" Coy? Yes, but she couldn't help but ask, and not just because of her curious inner kitty.

"Plenty where you're concerned, baby. And I am a man who likes to accomplish them."

He waggled his brows, and she laughed. "I have to admit I'm surprised you're only at #745."

"That's because every New Year I wipe my mission slate clean. I like to start the year fresh. Now, if you'll excuse me, I need to go attend to mission #747."

"Which is?"

"Take a cold shower and ease my blue balls before I totally cave to temptation."

"What if I wanted you to stay?"

He groaned and closed his eyes as he chanted, "Must not fail."

She laughed. "You're a strange man, Kyle."

"Strange, yet lovable?" he said, peering at her hopefully with one eye.

"Yes."

Apparently he liked her simple answer because he kissed her then, his arms wound tight enough to squeeze the breath from her. But she liked it, liked him, and hugged him back just as tight.

Then, just as she thought things might get interesting, he fled, still talking to her as he backed away, "Dammit, baby, you make a soldier forget himself. I'll be here to grab you both in the morning, and we're going to breakfast."

"Night, Rudolph!" she shouted as he hit the bottom step and the door to outside.

She laughed at his grumbled, "I still can't believe I'm doing that."

As she shut the door to her apartment, a stupid grin on her face, she couldn't help but hope this would be the best Christmas ever.

Chapter Seven

Worst. Christmas. Ever.

Blue-balled, squeaky clean, and twitchy from too much coffee, Kyle wondered at his sanity. *Why did I ever volunteer to do this? Can't someone find me a bomb to deactivate? Or demand I run cable for all the televisions in their house?*

It didn't help that his panicked urge to flee battled with an even stronger determination to stay, and all because of a certain cougar who sought to soothe his irritation.

"You look very handsome," Crystal purred in his ear as she stroked the fur between his antlers. "And don't worry. I'm sure the sparkles will probably fall off when you shift."

He gave her a dirty look, which given he wore a flashing red nose, did not intimidate her in the least.

"Poor, baby," she said with a laugh. "I'll have to make it up to you. Maybe after the parade you could come over for dinner."

He decided he wouldn't gore her with his tines.

"We can watch *Rise of the Guardians*."

A decent Christmas flick with lots of action. Don't judge him because he liked animated movies. Judge him because he knew the words to 'Let It Go' from *Frozen*.

"Then, once Gigi goes to bed, maybe you could…"

Yes. Yes.

"Help me wrap her presents. I suck when it comes to taping."

Big disappointment. His ears drooped, and she laughed.

"Ah, don't look so sad. I know it seems like a lot of work, but I'll make it worth your while. Promise," she said in a husky whisper.

With those teasing words, she sashayed away. If he could have wolf whistled, he would have. As it was, he did leer, in a caribou slobbery way. Then he growled and pawed the ground like a bull when he noticed he wasn't the only male appreciative of the view.

Mine. And he couldn't wait for the world—and most especially the males—to know it. Then, if they still dared leer, he'd show them why you never screwed with the guy who could scramble the password on their phone and not only change the outgoing voicemail message but also give it a really filthy, and loud, ringtone. One of his favorite pranks and best memories.

You could hear the moose bellow from a mile away.

Best part? Boris was inept when it came to technology and had to ask him nicely to help remove the offending tune.

Kyle marked the names and faces of the men who dared to admire what was his. Then mentally shook himself.

What am I doing?

Jealousy, never before experienced but recognizable. Just another sign Crystal was different than the other women he'd been with. *From now on, it will be only one woman.* While he'd certainly never expected to desire a domestic existence, ever since meeting Crystal and Gigi, it was all he could think of. All he wanted.

What I need.

It didn't take a mission to realize his life had been missing something since he'd returned from the war. He'd tried to fill that gaping hole with drinking, pranks, work, hell, he'd even started the occasional fight to see if hitting things would help.

Nothing had until now.

Crystal and Gigi, and the life he could so easily picture with them, fit perfectly in the void. They offered a chance at a happy life, a full life. A new existence he'd get to enjoy as soon as he got through the next hellish hour. An hour of torture he would surely never live down.

Luckily, no one in the staging area made fun of him in his ridiculous Rudolph getup.

Lucky because the parade was about to start and he didn't have time to wash the blood from his antlers if an idiot dared to mock him.

The parade starting, though, didn't mean he moved because he was, of course, leading the Santa sleigh, which meant he got to stand impatiently, in his harness, a herd of cow-like reindeer behind him and Earl the walrus practicing his ho-ho-ho's.

The floats moved out, one by one, lit with lights, garishly bright. The people of town, dressed in holiday regalia, moved out with them as Christmas music blared from speakers. The goodwill and cheer should have made him roll his eyes. Instead, he found it infectious. Next thing he knew, his hoof was tapping out the tune to 'Santa Claus is Coming to Town'.

Argh. Shoot me now. No. Don't. He couldn't fail in his mission for Gigi. She expected to see Rudolph, and by damn, she would, even if it killed him.

Goodbye, cruel world.

Time to accomplish Mission #746: Be the best fucking Rudolph ever for one little girl.

He held his head high. Antlers a glitter, his nose a brilliant flashing red. To the refrain of 'Rudolph', out he pranced, leading Santa's sleigh.

Only to balk at the door as panic suddenly overwhelmed him.

Everyone will see me.

They'll laugh.
They'll point.
They'll mock.
They'll...love me?

Caught just inside the door didn't mean he couldn't see some expectant faces, both young and old, as well as in between. And, yes, they bore smiles, but no smirks. He saw happy smiles that bespoke of a humor that was joyous, not taunting.

I survived the pit when I was in the army. I can survive this.

Out he stepped.

Jingle.

Step.

Jangle.

He began a steady walk, which caused the nickel-plated bells on his harness—no silver here—to ring.

After a few paces, he didn't pay attention anymore to his steps as he heard the delighted squeals and exclamations from the little ones present.

"Rudolph is leading the sleigh!"

"Look how big he is compared to the other reindeer."

"He's beautiful."

"Look at the size of his rack."

"Isn't he handsome?" said a familiar voice. Crystal's green eyes shone with thanks and affection.

As for Gigi, she didn't say a word, just stared at him with her bright gaze, her hands clasped in delight and her lips stretched in the biggest, happiest smile.

His chest swelled. *Oh yeah, mission accomplished.*

But she wasn't the only child wanting his attention. Hell, if he was going to do it, might as well do it right. He swung his glance to the other side of the road and let them glory in the best goddamned Rudolph they'd ever seen.

He pranced past Crystal and Gigi, following the marked parade route.

There was something crazily addictive, and, yes, fulfilling about being a part of the parade. Of bringing joy to others. Not that he'd ever admit it.

If his buddies asked how he liked playing Rudolph, he'd be sure to scratch his balls, say it was okay, and stress the fact that he'd done it for the children, not because it turned out he got a kick out of playing the part of a red-nosed freak.

Liking it, though, didn't mean he wasn't anxious to finish. As soon as they'd trotted the length of Main Street, back to the hangar they headed, Earl having disembarked out of sight of little faces, lest they realize Santa wasn't whom he seemed.

Forget following the others to the staging area. Kyle wanted out of this crazy getup and away from his crew—who seemed to think they could just poop whenever they wanted to. He thanked the fact he stayed ahead of the messes they left behind.

At least they obeyed. He led the mightily impressed reindeer at his back to the stable. They might be simple-minded, but they recognized greatness when they saw it. They respected his rack.

Crystal, minus one little girl, was there to meet him, a wide smile on her face. "You were awesome!"

Of course he was. He tossed his majestic head and, yes, struck a pose. If only Boris, who thought his set of antlers was so great, could have seen it. Kyle's might not yet have the span that ornery moose possessed, but his was sharper and more deadly.

He was also more handsome.

At least he hoped Crystal thought so as she stroked the fur behind his ears.

"Thank you," she said as she unhooked him from the traces.

Unable to reply, he snorted.

"Seriously. Gigi couldn't stop exclaiming about how good you looked. She barely even noticed Santa." Crystal laughed. "I think Kyle, the knight, might have competition."

His caribou seemed to find this mightily amusing. Kyle less so. *Wait until she sees what I got her for Christmas. She'll forget all about Rudolph then, pal.*

Jealous of himself? Ironic, but he could live with it.

Speaking of whom, where is my little sweetie? He made a questioning noise and swung his head side to side.

Crystal decoded his query. "I left her with the other children in the community center lest she realize a certain red nosed reindeer wasn't who he seemed."

Good plan. But it made him even more impatient to get unhitched so he could go find her. He wanted to hear firsthand—and yes bask—in her happiness that Rudolph had indeed saved the parade.

As Crystal worked at the leads holding him in the traces, he shuffled on his hooves. He couldn't wait to get the chafing leather straps off so he could shift back. He also couldn't wait to plant a kiss on Crystal. And watch some movies. And have the best Christmas ever.

He stood still as Crystal hummed a holiday melody, her nimble hands unbuckling as fast as she could.

They were alone out here, the rest of town having flowed into the community center for the Christmas party planned that night.

Yet even with the raucous sound of many shifters congregated not far away, and the blaring of tacky music, a small sound distracted him. A tiny cry he might have thought he imagined if not for the blanched expression on Crystal's face.

He didn't need her whispered "Gigi" to know his little sweetie needed him.

But where was she?

He angled his head and sniffed the air, not scenting a blasted thing, but once again he heard, or more like felt, Gigi's distress. Homing in on his target, much like a hound, off he took, bells jangling on the damned harness, nose flashing, a bull's-eye beacon to anyone targeting him. Let them.

Let whoever thought they could scare his sweetie see him coming and fear. Yes fear because he was going to gore the bastard and then trample him for his temerity.

For those who might wonder how a stranger might have slipped in to Kodiak Point and gotten close enough to snag a little girl, it was quite simple. There were a few times a year when strangers blended in and walked among them, mostly unnoticed. The summer months, when the curious tourists flocked while daylight reigned. At weddings, when wild cousins and city ones gathered for a good time. And then there was Christmas, when families and clans and all kinds of shifters came visiting from around the world to spend the holidays together.

So was it difficult for a certain stupid wolf—who'd surely suffered some brain damage, probably from sniffing too much glue—to slip in during the chaos and think to abscond with a precious little girl?

My little girl.

A little girl he would save. Kyle didn't need to declare a mission in this case. He'd already made a promise, and he would keep it.

He wasn't alone in his chase. A sleek cougar, her fur a rich gold, bounded ahead of him, still wearing shreds of clothes and...was that a red lace thong? Damn. He would have loved to have torn that off Crystal himself later on. But, no, a certain ex-boyfriend just had to show up and ruin Kyle's excellent evening.

Someone has a death wish.

A wish he would grant. With Kyle thundering on four hooves through a town he knew too well, Malcolm wouldn't get far.

But he tried.

Malcolm made it to his truck, parked not far from the ravine, before he whirled around, Gigi in his grasp, her eyes wide with fright.

So unacceptable.

Kyle let out a bellow. Crystal snarled.

Malcom, his eyes wild and bloodshot, his longish dark hair standing every which way, didn't seem to care. "Stop where you are, or the girl gets it," he threatened.

What kind of prick threatened a child?

A dead one.

Given the peril to Gigi, Kyle halted, but he pawed the ground, his breath steaming from his nostrils, his muscles clenching and ready for him to spring into action.

He wasn't alone. Crystal padded slowly toward Malcolm, rumbling a warning growl, which went well with the lip she pulled back in a snarl. A vicious cougar ready to protect her cub.

"Stop right there," Malcolm threatened. "I mean it. And tell your freaky deer buddy to go away or I will hurt her."

Deer? Hello, someone needed to brush up on his terminology because Kyle was a caribou and a buck. Which rhymed with *I'm going to kill that fuck.*

I'm a poet, and I didn't even know it.

A gun appeared in Malcolm's hand, and Kyle's blood turned cold as the situation escalated. Forget jokes, or rash actions, he needed to focus and act.

The weapon froze Crystal in her tracks. She shifted back to her human form and failed to stifle her frightened sob. "Don't," she cried, her bare skin pebbling in the cold. "I'll do whatever you want. Just don't hurt her."

Kyle hated to hear her plead with the prick.

"Tell him to go away." Malcolm swung the gun at Kyle. "This is none of his business."

Crystal shot him a frantic look that both asked him to leave and, at the same time, begged him for help.

Leaving wouldn't solve anything, so Kyle stood his ground, a fact Malcolm noticed.

"Great. A fucking moron. They seem to be everywhere this year." He sneered. "I always wanted a rack to mount on my wall."

Under the right circumstance, like now, caribou could and would growl. Kyle lowered his head and pawed the ground, daring him to try.

It was then that the light bulb, which wasn't very bright, went off in the idiot's head. "Wait a second. I know your scent. If it isn't the teddy bear lover who thinks he's a fucking hero. Anxious for a bullet, are you?"

Not really. Bullets stung, and he'd know. Kyle even had the scars to prove it. But he could handle getting shot if it got him close enough to take care of the prick. *Or at least within reach of my antlers.*

Poor sweet, deluded Crystal. She still thought she could negotiate with the insane jerk.

"You can't expect to get away with this, Malcolm. Let Gigi go."

He gripped her tighter which in turn made Gigi whimper.

He was surprised his simmering anger didn't steam from his ears.

Just give me an opening, you bastard.

Malcolm didn't hear the silent request and kept Gigi as a shield. "Why would I let her go? She's my ticket to keeping you in line. I know you. I know how much you love this brat. So, when I say to get your ass in the truck or else, I know you'll listen if you don't want her to get hurt."

The inability to act, burned. If only he could get Gigi away from the insane bastard, then he could take care of the jerk. *I have to do something. I must rescue her.* It drove him into a dark place he'd not visited in a long time to feel so helpless.

He won't win. I won't let him. Hang on, sweetie. I'll think of something.

Crystal still tried to reason, but her fear rolled off her in palpable waves. "Malcolm, you can't seriously think you can just waltz out of here with me and Gigi as hostages. The clan won't stand for it."

"They will if they want you both to stay alive. Now stop your jabbering and get over here. Now!"

"No."

It wasn't Crystal that said it, nor Kyle, who still wore his majestic—yet currently useless—form. The tiny no came from a little girl. A little girl who, while scared out of her mind, stood up to the bully.

"No." She said it louder and then sank her teeth into Malcolm's arm.

Nothing like a pair of sharp cub teeth sinking into flesh to make a tough guy scream like a girl. Malcolm let out a high-pitched holler and thrust the little girl from him.

Just what Kyle wanted.

He charged in while Crystal, still naked—except for that damnable thong—darted to Gigi.

Bang.

Oh no.

It should have been him. Why was the idiot not focused on him? *I need to really work on mission #732* because perhaps had his reputation preceded him then Malcolm would have aimed the gun Kyle's way. But no, the sick stalker aimed at Crystal, who, intent on reaching Gigi, couldn't even dodge. The bullet hit her high in the thigh, and she yelped in pain as she crumpled to the ground.

Then Kyle lost track of her as his tines hit Malcolm, sank into soft flesh and hit a few major arteries. Malcolm didn't even manage to utter one last squeak. As soon as Kyle had him impaled, he heaved the dying wolf in the air.

People often wondered how strong a caribou rack truly was. How deadly. Well, given Kyle was able to hoist Malcolm on his pointed spires and trot with him over to a certain ravine that cut through the town, and all without effort, anyone could conclude his rack was built to wreak havoc. It was also great for tossing the carcass of a pesky wolf that had stalked his last victim down to a watery death in the icy current.

Would he regret his actions later? Feel remorse?

Nah. Welcome to a shifter's world. Rules existed to keep them in line and to keep their existence secret. Break them and there was no lengthy trial, no jury. Just swift and final justice.

For a man who thought it was okay to threaten a little girl and her mother? There was no second chance. Not in Kyle's world.

Goodbye, Malcolm.

A cry caught his attention.

"Gigi, come back."

Off he trotted, back to where he'd left his girls, but although he'd been gone only for a few minutes, it was only Crystal who sat slumped on the ground, hands pressed over a bloody swath of skin.

"Kyle," she said through gritted teeth. "It's Gigi. She's run off and I can't follow because of my damned leg."

Such a tough cougar, bitching about getting shot rather than the fact that she sat in just a thong—a thong that taunted—in the fucking snow. At least she wouldn't suffer for long. Kyle could hear the shouts of clan folk as they ran their way, the gunshot having drawn their attention.

Knowing Crystal would soon have all the help—and clothes—she needed, Kyle took off in search of one lost little girl.

Lucky for him, Gigi kept her human shape because, had she shifted in to a nimble cat, he might not have found it easy to follow, especially if she'd clambered in to the trees lining the ravine's edge. Her little snowbooted steps proved easy to trail, and he had no fear of startling her, not with those damnable bells on his harness still jingling.

Oh, and he wasn't going to discuss the flashing red nose that had managed to hang on during the entire ordeal.

He'd just begun to wonder if he'd ever catch up to her—little or not, the kid could move!—when he caught sight of movement. Now keep in mind that given the darkness and fir trees, light wasn't exactly abundant, and his eyesight wasn't as great as his rack. So Kyle held himself ready, one hoof lifted, rack slightly inclined, ready to dash or charge, depending on what lumbered from the shadows.

This time of the year, all kinds of nasty beasties roamed, usually not this close to town, but one never knew. The abominable snowman did so enjoy hyping the rumors of his existence. Now *there* was a beast who didn't need help with his reputation.

So, given what Kyle knew of the dark and its hidden possibilities, he held himself at the ready. But, in this case, what flew at him was a pink cutie who came hurtling from behind the safety of some branches, threw herself at him, and hugged his neck as far as she could reach.

"You found me."

Well, duh, of course I did.

"You saved me."

Hell yeah.

"I like your red nose."

Oh crap, she thinks I'm Rudolph.

"Love you, Kyle."

No. Oh no. Caribou do not cry. They blink nonexistent snowflakes from their eyes. They sniffle because they have a cold, but they do not cry. Ack. Argh. Sigh. Kyle melted like a marshmallow over a lit butane torch.

Okay, so he was a tiny bit touched by her words. He nosed her arm and then licked her cheek.

She giggled. "Ew, I like real kisses better."

He made a noise and waggled his head, kind of shy about shifting back. It was one thing to appear naked in front of Crystal and other grown women, another to do it in front of a little girl.

Luckily, Gigi was as smart as she was cute. She understood the situation, but then she really tested his affection for her when she clambered up his broad side, using the straps holding the damned harness with bells on.

When she perched herself astride his back, he couldn't move, mostly out of shock.

Help! Someone's trying to ride my majestic beast! Not just someone. Gigi.

For her, he would allow the ignoble gesture—but gore anyone who remarked on it.

Nobody else wanted to die that night apparently because nothing was said other than a happy "Munchkin!" when Crystal caught sight of her daughter.

After that, things got a little wild as the town swept them in their tide and brought them back to the center, where someone gave him some clothes—which included a fugly Christmas sweater—and the doctor patched Crystal's leg and told her to take it easy.

Mission #748: No stairs for Crystal.

Like he needed an excuse to carry her. Hell, he carried both his girls up the steep flight to their apartment when they finally managed to escape the busy community center for somewhere a little more quiet.

After a shower parade, where they all sluiced the day's events from their skin and dressed—him in an early gift from Crystal of Rudolph-patterned flannel pants and a shirt imprinted with a fat Santa that said "Poke me and die!"—they sat down to eat a frozen pizza they'd cooked in the oven—cheese only of course—plus a giant salad. They watched a Christmas flick, and then Kyle got to help tuck Gigi in.

A hug and a sloppy kiss were given to Crystal. "Night, Mama."

"Night, munchkin." Crystal hugged her daughter tight and kissed her a few times before releasing her and making room for Kyle.

He perched himself on the side of the bed and obeyed when a pair of wee arms stretched out demandingly.

"Night, Kyle."

He also got a wet, smacking kiss on the cheek. Damn cold. He sniffled. "Night, sweetie," he murmured in a husky tone because of his clogged—surely getting sore—throat.

He went to lay her down, but she wasn't done.

"Do you think Santa will find me?" she whispered, her eyes almost shut.

"I'll make sure he does, even if I have to hang that bright flashing nose from the chimney," Kyle promised.

Mission #749: Find a ladder.

He left before he made any more outrageous promises.

Crystal laughed as she shut the door. "You know she thinks she has you wrapped around her baby finger."

"What do you mean thinks? She totally does," he boasted with a big smile.

As Crystal chuckled, Kyle carried his cougar to the couch, conscious of his duty to keep her from stressing her leg until it healed, which, given her shifter gene, wouldn't take long. By morning, it would appear as a fresh scar.

As the mobile one, it was up to him to gather the few bags of presents, wrapping paper, tape, and scissors. It seemed Crystal had not jested when she said they'd wrap.

As he wadded his fiftieth piece of sticky tape, he admitted defeat. "And this is why I pay someone to wrap things for me."

"Tell you what. I'll wrap, and you sit there looking pretty."

He ogled her. "Why do I feel complimented and insulted all at once?"

An impish smile curved her lips. "Because I'm that good."

Indeed she was. With only the gentle glow of a lamp and the sparkling ones off the ugly tree, which wasn't as ugly now that Kyle was used to it, he could finally claim relief, relief that the day, while tumultuous, had ended up turning out okay after all.

When Crystal placed the last present under the tree, Kyle noted a decoration on her battered coffee table. The thing looked ancient, and for some reason, Kyle grabbed it for a closer look. He fingered the tattered Santa, the red velvet of its suit worn smooth in spots, but the rosy painted cheeks and the mischievous twinkle in the eye were standing well against the test of time. Unlike poor Saint Nick's hand-held little bell. Made of a shiny golden-colored metal, it didn't ring.

Turning it around in his hands, Kyle found a switch on the bottom and flicked it. Nothing, He shook it. Poked it. But nothing he did got the chubby red man to ring his bell.

"Don't bother," Crystal said as she leaned away from the tree to nestle herself against him—where she belonged. "He hasn't worked in years."

"So why keep him?"

"He originally belonged to my great-grandma, so I guess that makes him a family heirloom. When I graduated and things started going to hell for me, she gave him to me because he was supposed to bring good luck."

"Kind of like a rabbit's foot?"

"I guess, except we didn't use him to make wishes. The way he's supposed to work, or did, was every Christmas Eve, before bed, Nana and I would poke him in his fat belly. He'd say "Ho! Ho! Ho!" and ring his little bell. When he did that, Nana said that meant we'd have a year of good luck."

"When did he stop working?" he asked, even if he could guess.

"He hasn't spoken or rung his bell since the year I got pregnant and Nana died." She uttered a chuckle tinged with a touch of bitterness. "I guess he's my version of a broken mirror. But enough of sad things in the past. Tonight is Christmas Eve. A time of goodwill and all that stuff. A time for new beginnings," she murmured against his neck before placing a kiss.

Which turned into a suck.

Which turned into him lying on his back, her sprawled across him and necking like people in love.

The L word should have frightened him. The last time he'd thought himself in love he had been betrayed in the worst possible way. But Crystal wasn't like that. She wasn't fickle. She would stay true. Especially once he got her trust and love.

Mine.

A claim he must have murmured out loud because she whispered back, "Yes, yours."

Say what you would, there was something wickedly sexy about a woman you'd set your sights on admitting aloud she belonged to you. It made a man want to truly claim her. Not just in body but soul.

If there was such a thing as a mate bond, Kyle was going to find it, right here, right now, with this woman.

The only thing that gave him pause was her injury. He'd have to take her gently, even if she seemed intent on ignoring her wound.

She growled as he kissed her sensually and let his hands roam the skin hidden by her pajama top. "Would you stop pussyfooting and make love to me, dammit."

"First off, I hoof it. Second, yes, ma'am." What could he say? He was a man who liked direct orders, especially when they aligned with his own desires.

It wasn't long before they were skin to skin. Except for one itsy bitty item.

"You tease me all day with memories of a thong, and you wear these now?" he grumbled as he caught sight of her panties. White cotton and, on the front, a certain happy reindeer.

"But they glow in the dark."

Seriously?

This he had to see. Off went the lamp, but he didn't need to figure out how to switch off the tree because the room was dark enough for him to see the bright red circle.

"Crystal, with your panties so bright, won't you guide my—"

"Don't you dare say it," she interrupted with a laugh.

"Fine, but I'm thinking it." He sat on the couch beside her and gathered her into his arms. She fit perfectly. Soft skin, lush curves, a berry scent that made his mouth water.

Their lips found each other and slid with a passion no longer content to go slow. Need built. Urgency throbbed.

As did his shaft.

He grunted when she slid a hand between their bodies and grasped him, the tip of her thumb brushing the pearl drop at the head. With slow strokes, she petted him, the smooth glide of her hand on his cock making him hiss as he struggled to hold on.

How he wanted her.

His fingers threaded through her hair as he dragged her in for a rough kiss. Hungrily, he devoured her mouth and sucked at her tongue. Their steamy pants bespoke their rising excitement.

"I want you, Kyle," she murmured, the soft wind of her words sending a shiver through him.

"I need you," he admitted. *I think I love you.*

She froze.

Uh-oh. I think I said that aloud.

Chapter Eight

"I think I love you."

Given the way Kyle froze—a buck caught in headlights—she assumed she'd not misheard him. She also guessed he'd not meant to say it aloud. At least not yet.

The tenseness of his body hinted he might flee. The poor guy, he'd already bent so much. It took a strong man, a decent man, to vanquish his vanity to please a little girl. It took a man with courage to come to their rescue. It took a man in love to allow himself to be assimilated, um, she meant domesticated, and in such a short span.

Her poor knight. She let him have a break and saved him. "I think I love you, too."

"You do?"

"Are you that surprised?"

"Hell no. I just thought it would take longer for you to realize my greatness."

"Greatness?" She practically choked—with laughter.

Only he could shoot her an unrepentant grin and get away with it. "Admit it. It was the rack. Impressive, eh? And Boris thinks his set of antlers is so hot. Ha. Everyone knows caribous do it better."

Crystal couldn't help herself. She fell over snickering. And then yowling.

Then laughing as Kyle attacked her with tickling fingers.

"I'll teach you to laugh at me," he grumbled.

Funny how much she enjoyed his *punishment*.

Despite their mirthful interruption, the passion returned quickly and with a vengeance. Tickles turned to caresses. Caresses turned to panties getting torn off. Naked pussy was faced with a hard shaft.

Mmm. *Lucky me, Christmas is coming early. Make that Crystal is coming. Maybe more than once.*

Kyle sheathed himself within her, thick, hot, and hard. He stretched her, filled her, touched her, and she loved it. She arched below him, legs splayed wide, giving him deep access.

As he pumped in and out of her, she clawed at his back, his shoulders, anything she could grasp that would bring him closer.

And closer.

They kissed as their bodies moved in rhythm, his thrusts welcomed by her tightening sex. The hardness of his strokes striking her G-spot heightened her coiling pleasure. With a soft cry of his name, bliss rolled over her. Her muscles spasmed and milked his throbbing cock until he spurted hotly within her. Marking her as surely as if he'd placed a ring around her finger. Claiming her with his seed and his words, "Mine."

However, Crystal was a little more traditional when it came to mating. And she was, after all, a carnivore. They liked things a bit more permanent, and rough. She bit him, high on the shoulder, not savagely, but firm enough to break skin.

To his credit, he only hissed and didn't complain. He understood what she did. The trust she placed in him. His second, "Mine," emerged deeper, huskier.

He gathered her in his arms and arranged them in a sitting position on the couch, holding her close, her head tucked under his chin.

She'd never been more content.

Which was why she made a sound of protest when he dumped her on the cushion beside him and said, "Shit, I almost forgot."

Forgot what?

Whatever it was, it required him throwing on some pants and barreling down the stairs. He returned moments later laden with gifts. One, a box covered in silver shiny paper with a big red bow, caught Crystal's eye.

"What's in that one?" she asked as she pointed.

"You'll have to wait and see, my curious kitty."

"It's for me?" The concept flummoxed her. Sure, she'd gotten him the pajama set when she grabbed some groceries before the parade—having left him and Gigi in charge of last-minute float fixes—but she'd grabbed the garments more as a joke. This, though, looked planned.

"Yes, it's for you, baby. Gigi helped me pick it."

Hearing that, the love she felt growing for him got even bigger. "I can see how this is going to work," she teased. "You and the munchkin in cahoots against me."

"Join us," he said with a leer, "we have access to freshly baked cookies."

"Ah, but I have the pie," she teased, leaning back against the couch, her smile an invitation.

How she loved a man with stamina. Most especially this man. A man who'd given her the best Christmas she ever recalled. Her caribou's gift? Love and trust.

And, finally, my very own happily ever after.

Epilogue

Waking up Christmas morning beside the woman he loved? Awesome.

Having a squealing little girl fly into the room, soar onto the bed, and land on his balls? It brought a tear to his eye—and almost had him utter an unmanly whimper.

But he wasn't upset. How could he be when Gigi shone with such obvious happiness, not at all perturbed by the fact he'd slept in her mother's bed—a bed he planned to share every night. Which reminded him…

Mission #750: Get a cup to wear to bed.

Mission #751: Remember to also wear underpants.

As Gigi gushed about the presents under the tree, he couldn't help but smile, mostly because Crystal snuggled against him—the smart woman having donned a nightgown at some point during the night.

Heat warmed his cheeks when she drew the covers back to slide out of bed. Kyle scrambled for the linen, intent on keeping his manparts covered.

A smirk appeared on Crystals face, the wench not at all repentant at making a tough soldier blush. "Hey, munchkin, what do you say you and I go take a peek at the stash under the tree? Mama also needs to get some coffee started."

"But what about Kyle?" Gigi asked, craning to peek back at him.

"Kyle's coming. He just needs to, uh…"

"Pee?" Gigi added helpfully.

No amount of training in the army could prepare a man for that kind of guilelessness.

Crystal snorted as Kyle wished for a hole he could hide in.

As the ladies left the room, Kyle found his pajama pants and slid them on, along with the fugly Christmas sweater he'd borrowed the night before. Might as well go all out.

He'd have to see about getting his clothes brought over. Hopefully Crystal had some room for him to stash them. Or maybe they should think about just getting a bigger place for all of them to share.

Crystal might not know it yet, but he was here to stay. He'd meant what he said to her the night before. Short courtship or not, she was his soul mate, and he loved her. Real love based on more than looks or sex. Crystal made him want things in life, a home, a family, a future. Time to start a legacy and traditions. Or continue a tradition in this case.

Almost giant teddy time.

For those who didn't know, Kyle's dad had served in the military, which meant he didn't control when he was home or away. His father couldn't always ensure he'd be home in time for Christmas, but no matter where he was in the world, Kyle knew when he got up Christmas morning, the biggest freaking stuffed animal would have its furry ass under the tree. It became a tradition until Kyle enlisted and his dad said he was too old for giant stuffies. Kyle disagreed, but no matter. The time had finally come for him to take up the giant teddy challenge.

Just one problem, Crystal's tree wasn't big enough to accommodate it—this year, but he had plans for the next.

But first, they needed to take care of the gifts already under the tree. As he and Crystal sipped coffee on the couch, Gigi doled wrapped packages out, one by one.

For some reason, he got to open his first.

"That one's from me," Gigi announced, as he eyed the lumpy package.

Eager to see what it held, he tore at the wrapping, then couldn't help but laugh at the multi-pack of Hubba Bubba.

"You remembered," he said, as Gigi beamed.

"Of course she did. According to my daughter, you blow the biggest bubbles ever."

He winked at Crystal. "Baby, I do everything bigger."

The blush on her cheeks? Adorable. He couldn't help but drop a light kiss on her lips.

More presents were opened including the one he'd gotten for Crystal.

Crystal pulled out the slippers, a puzzled look on her face. "Are these the donkey from Shrek?"

"They are. Your daughter said you needed them for your feet."

At Crystal's puzzled glance, Gigi sighed and rolled her eyes. "Don't you remember, mama? You said you needed a donkey for your foot."

Crystal bit her lip and managed a choked, "That's right, munchkin. I did."

"Mind explaining?" Kyle asked as Gigi went on to open her next gift.

Crystal leaned close and whispered, "I, uh, might have gotten a tad upset one day and said I needed to put my foot up an ass."

Kyle didn't bother to hold in his laughter, a mirth Crystal shared.

Actually the whole morning was filled with chuckles and smiles. Except for when Crystal finally opened the other gift he got her, which was more like a gift for him. Despite her red cheeks when Gigi remarked it didn't look too warm, Crystal promised to model it later that night. *Best Christmas ever!*

Once all the gifts were unwrapped, it was time for Gigi's final surprise. As the girls discussed the merits of pancakes versus waffles for breakfast, Kyle sneaked out to his truck parked outside.

When he returned, they'd moved on to arguing real maple syrup versus the brown sugar kind. He plopped the huge panda, with a wee modification, down on the floor.

"Kyle, what are you doing?" Crystal exclaimed.

"Bringing Gigi her last gift." Like duh.

"It's for me?" Gigi's smile lit up the room.

He waggled the giant bear, with its fabric set of antlers sewn to its crown, at her. "Of course. And, look, I made it more handsome."

"Indeed he did," Crystal said with a smile as she laced her arm in his and leaned her head on his shoulder.

As for Gigi, she hugged the big teddy, which was almost as huge as her.

Mission accomplished, he sat on the couch and yanked Crystal down onto his lap. The living room was a mess of paper, just like it should be Christmas morning.

All the gifts were open, or so he thought, until he noted a bright red corner peeking from behind the tree.

Crystal spotted it at about the same time he did. "Another one? Spoiling her?"

"Well yeah, except that one isn't from me."

"Well, it's not from me."

As they stared at each other in puzzlement, Gigi wandered over to the mysterious gift and pulled it out. Her chubby finger traced the letters on the ornate gold-embossed tag.

"To, Gigi," she read. "Fr-o-m, Santa."

Kyle glanced at Crystal, who shrugged, but before he could dive on the present and pull it from Gigi—his military training not liking the unidentified package—the little girl had torn the paper to shreds.

They didn't blow up, but their eardrums practically burst at the squeal.

"It's the Lego Friends Mall," Gigi screamed. "Santa did bring it, Mama. Look!"

Crystal muttered, "Did you do this?"

He shook his head. "I wish I could take the credit, but I couldn't find it anywhere."

"But…" Crystal couldn't seem to find the words to complete her sentence.

And it didn't help that the plastic Santa on the table chose that moment, dead batteries or not, to utter "Ho-Ho-Ho, Merry Christmas."

The hairs on his arms raised, but Kyle didn't take a gun to the haunted holiday figure. But he would if his ladies didn't get their year of good luck.

A few days later…

The second hand hit midnight, and the New Year rang in to the raucous howls of shifters gone wild partying. Kyle and Crystal opted for something a little more intimate—and naked.

As he kissed her and ushered in the New Year, he wiped the mission slate clean and then immediately planned his first, and most important task ever.

Mission #1: *Love and protect my family.*
Forever.

* * *

You know Boris and Travis, and Brody and Reid,
Guys who kick butt and go to extremes.
But do you recall,
The most vain ex-soldier of all?

Kyle, the technical specialist,
Had a very impressive rack.
And if you ever see it,
Run if he screams "Attack!"

All of his sworn enemies,
Thought that they could call him names,
So he pinned them with his rack
And made them scream until death came.

Then one cold-ass Christmas Eve,

Crystal came and said,
"You pompous jerk, I hate your guts
If you think I'll date you, then you're nuts."

Kyle suddenly saw the light,
And agreed to do what it would take.
That's when he learned that playing a reindeer,
Could result in some sensual games.

The next exciting **Kodiak Point story, Wolf's Capture,** features Brody and a mystery lady. More info at EveLanglais.com

www.ingramcontent.com/pod-product-compliance
Lightning Source LLC
LaVergne TN
LVHW012114070526
838202LV00056B/5732